The Bordea

The Bo

CW01460953

Connection

John Paul Davis

John Paul Davis
The Bordeaux Connection
Fourth Edition (2023)

The Bordeaux Connection

For The Originals

John Paul Davis
Praise for JPD

Can't wait for the new one . . .
Richard Doetsch, international bestselling author of *The Thieves of Heaven*

I found this an enjoyable read, with different subplots and an exciting historical treasure hunt all coming together to make a satisfying novel. The history in the novel was very well researched, and I was particularly thrilled to see a few mentions of Henry of Grosmont, first duke of Lancaster (c. 1310-61), a hero of mine!
Kathryn Warner, UK #1 Bestselling History Author

If John Paul Davis wrote the phonebook, we'd all be reading it!
Keith Houghton, #1 bestselling thriller author

Takes you on a fast-paced, thoroughly researched thrill ride . . .
David Leadbeater, #1 bestselling thriller author and winner of the Amazon Storytelling Award

. . . fascinating, action-packed thriller melding past, present and future.
Karen Perkins, international bestselling thriller author and winner of the silver medal for European Fiction in the 2015 Independent Publisher Book Awards

John Paul Davis clearly owns the genre of historical thrillers!
Steven Sora, author of *The Lost Colony of the Templars*

. . . well-researched, original and fascinating . . .
Graham Phillips, international bestselling non-fiction author

Prepare for the most fascinating read you'll get in ages
The Birmingham Post

The Bordeaux Connection
Books by John Paul Davis

Thrillers

The Templar Agenda
The Larmenius Inheritance
The Plantagenet Vendetta
The Cromwell Deception (a prequel to The Crown Jewels
Conspiracy)
The Bordeaux Connection (a White Hart prequel)
The Cortés Trilogy: Enigma, Revenge, Revelation (The Complete
Ben Maloney Series)
The Crown Jewels Conspiracy (The White Hart #1)
The Rosicrucian Prophecy (The White Hart #2)
The Excalibur Code (The White Hart #3)
The Merlin Stone (The White Hart #4)
The Lost Crowns (The White Hart #5)
The Chaucer Manuscript (The White Hart #6)

Historical Non-Fiction

Robin Hood: The Unknown Templar (Peter Owen Publishers)
Pity For The Guy – a Biography of Guy Fawkes (Peter Owen
Publishers)
The Gothic King – a Biography of Henry III (Peter Owen
Publishers)
A Hidden History of the Tower of London – England's Most
Notorious Prisoners (Pen & Sword History)
King John, Henry III and England's Lost Civil War (Pen & Sword
History)
Castles of England (Pen & Sword History)
Castles of Wales (Pen & Sword History)

For more information, please visit www.officiallyjpd.com

John Paul Davis
The White Hart Series

The Bordeaux Connection (a White Hart prequel)
The Crown Jewels Conspiracy (The White Hart #1)
The Rosicrucian Prophecy (The White Hart #2)
The Excalibur Code (The White Hart #3)
The Merlin Stone (The White Hart #4)
The Lost Crowns (The White Hart #5)
The Chaucer Manuscript (The White Hart #6)

The Bordeaux Connection

In medieval England, the defence of the realm in times of need rested on the shoulders of twelve knights – a secret order who swore to protect the people at all costs . . .

They were called the White Hart . . .

As they are now . . .

John Paul Davis
Shamed be the person who thinks evil of it
Edward III of England

The Bordeaux Connection
Prologue

Bordeaux, France
14:57, Monday 19 March

The old man watched from the window as the cars began to leave. Each one was identical; limousines of the same type had been in his family for over a decade, though the models were upgraded every few years. It was a neighbourhood where the residents demanded it – where even the slightest blemish on a car door could irreparably damage one's reputation. The same was true of the drivers. Each had been handpicked for specific reasons, the ability to drive being only one of them. None of them were inexperienced in dealing with those of status, nor were they foolish enough to enquire into such a person's business when it didn't concern them.

Like the cars, they were renowned for their discretion and efficiency.

As the final limousine departed the winding driveway, heading back onto the long avenue close to the banks of the Garonne, the old man shuffled away from the window and took in the features of the well-lit room. The recent meeting had gone to plan, as they usually did when only the closest family was present. Eighty years had taught him much about the business world; a man could work with the same people for years, only to find those he trusted most had been twisting a knife in his back since day one. A boss could pay for many services and be met with varying results.

In a business where both trust and quality were paramount, he employed only those dearest to him.

As he moved about the deserted room, the upstairs of the chateau adjusting to the new quietness, he found himself replaying recent conversations in his mind. The chances of carrying out the dream of a lifetime depended solely on the successful acquisition of three important things.

The first would be found in England, in an estate once associated with a family of similar prestige.

The second would be found in the capital of Scotland, somewhere among the official archives.

The third, perhaps most importantly, would be found closer to home, on the walls of a famous museum.

Each endeavour would be conducted independently; success in one would not guarantee success in the others. Worse, failure in one could end everything. Only with all three could the dream be fully accomplished.

Leaving the luxurious room, he saw from the face of the grandfather clock on the landing it was precisely 15:00. If all went to plan, the first of the men would be leaving the city now, catching a plane to England.

Once successful, they would find their own way north.

Edinburgh, Scotland
23:07

If there are enemies on the left and enemies on the right, which way do you go?

The man from Bordeaux knew he had a decision to make. The ancient room that had been filled with smoke seconds earlier, restricting his vision and causing his breathing to shorten, was now swarming with armed guards, its historic walls echoing with the sound of footsteps. Though he was still to see or hear gunfire, he knew it wouldn't take long for that to come. Time was precious.

As were the items he'd come for.

Further reinforcements were arriving from two winding stairways, clearly announced by the consistent dull thuds of heavy boots on stone. Accompanying them, short military commands barked out over a dozen radio headsets that crackled in the building's acoustics. Though the smoke had largely dispersed,

The Bordeaux Connection

visibility was limited, and the faces of the newcomers were deep in shadow. In the dim light of the cold heavy stone surroundings, sounds seemed to intensify, heightening the growing feeling of anticipation that had been building steadily in the pit of the Frenchman's stomach. In seconds it would begin.

Enemies on the left. Enemies on the right. Which way to go? He made his decision.

The way with fewer enemies.

A thunderous crash pierced the vaults, the fourth in the last forty seconds. The first had occurred above ground at the east end of the Royal Mile, ten seconds before the second, half a mile to the west. Ten seconds after that came a third, exactly ten seconds before the most recent. Being underground, the Frenchman hadn't witnessed the sights, but the noises left him in no doubt that the eruptions had been severe. The news he was getting through his earpiece confirmed that all four had been executed on schedule.

So far, the plan had gone off perfectly.

The gunfire started within seconds of the fourth explosion. A series of ear-splitting roars erupted from both doorways. Bright flashes from semi-automatic weapons preceded a constant barrage of heavy fire that peppered the walls.

Instinctively, he dived to his right. In the underground archive, the only available cover was a sophisticated racking system whose contents dated back through history. Although the setting was as he had anticipated from the information he had obtained prior to arrival, he still found it hard to believe such a place could exist in the 21st century. Throughout his career, he had observed many vaulted rooms located below ground in the capital cities of Europe, but what he saw now was unlike any he could recall. It was primitive yet futuristic. Efficient but elaborate.

The average citizen could walk the famous road above, passing in and out of its famous classical buildings, and never know what existed just twenty metres below them.

Staying low, he darted behind one of the racks.

"*Quelle direction?*" he bellowed at the nearest of his three accomplices, his voice partially drowned out by gunfire. *Which way?*

The man next to him was of almost identical appearance: short black hair and a dark combat uniform representing no one organisation or country. "Up. The stairs are the only way."

The Frenchman cursed his luck, quietly unsurprised. The vault had been explicitly designed to keep priceless objects safe.

Not to facilitate a quick exit.

As the room fell quiet, he returned fire at the left stairway, the bullets causing sparks to bounce off the stonework. No explosions had occurred beneath the ground, nor would they. The smoke that had recently filled the far side of the chamber, forming quickly and dissipating like a passing river mist, had been a deliberate masking tactic. Setting off explosives underground was unthinkable. The foundation walls were far too old to take such a risk.

One mistake, and it would be game over.

More enemies were descending the left stairwell, their movements clearly audible. The man from Bordeaux replaced another magazine on his Uzi submachine gun and fired wildly at the latest movements. Amidst the gunfire, he heard people screaming, their cries of anguish echoing off the nearby rocky surroundings.

Without warning, the room became darker. What little light had entered through the far doorways had been extinguished – he guessed deliberately. As he retreated further into the heart of the archive, he activated the night-vision setting on his goggles. Guards advanced from both stairways, more than twenty in total – outnumbering him and his men by five to one. From headwear to boots, their appearance was immaculate. Scotland's finest was out in force; he estimated perhaps half the entire roster.

Nevertheless, experience told him whatever covert personnel the UK government was blessed with, the cream would probably not be present in Scotland's capital.

The Bordeaux Connection

He fired, concentrating on the enemies who had appeared on the left side while keeping low behind the metallic shelving units as the enemy returned fire in force. As his ammunition magazine ran low, he heard a loud warning behind him. He saw his accomplice's arm move in a pendulum motion: a round grenade-like object left his hand and launched toward the stairways. It exploded on hitting the ground, the sounds softer than before.

Within seconds the room filled with smoke.

The smoke took longer to clear than on the previous occasions; he estimated thirty seconds. When it did, he saw nothing but stillness – more than a dozen bodies lying in a heap.

Slowly he approached, satisfied the potency of the gas had worn off. In the silence, he noticed his ears were ringing, his skin patchy with sweat. As he adjusted to the quiet, new truths dawned on him.

Outside, the explosions had also ceased.

He turned to his accomplices; all were still alive, each carrying a large holdall filled to the limit with artwork and historical manuscripts.

"*Quelle destination maintenant? La gauche ou la droite?*" he asked. *Where to now? The left or the right?*

The man alongside him rubbed his beard, his eyes still piercing with aggression. In the briefing, he learned that the upper part of the vault was more modern than the rest of the building, albeit still over five centuries old.

"*La Gauche,*" he replied, pointing to the left stairwell. "The tunnel ends after two hundred metres; it will take us into the grounds of the old abbey."

The man from Bordeaux nodded and checked his watch. "Ten seconds. Remember, whatever happens. This," he removed one particular article from the man's bag, "must return home at all costs. The fate of our mission depends on this."

Though no further words were said, the message was clearly understood. The small window of opportunity between the discovery and the raised alarm had been enough to confirm the facts. The item was old, early 15th century, and marked with the correct insignias.

The chances of forgery or human error were slight.

The leader of the four ascended the left stairwell and continued along the tunnel. Its appearance was similar to the vaults below. Arched and walled, with a glimmer of light coming from the far end. In his mind, he counted down the seconds: four, three, two, one . . .

A fifth explosion, the loudest yet. It appeared to come from directly behind them. Again the surroundings shook violently, causing his legs to buckle.

Retaining his balance, he sprinted to the end of the tunnel, where the light was brighter, making his night-vision goggles redundant. He finally emerged into the night air and was greeted by the smell of wet grass and the sound of nearby traffic.

Amongst the smells and sounds, he sensed screaming and burning.

The Bordeaux Connection
1

Peterhead, Scotland,
23:07, Tuesday 20 March

The mission ended in Peterhead, a small port on the east coast of Scotland. It had begun twenty-four hours earlier, one hundred and fifty miles south in Edinburgh. The catalyst was a terrorist attack: five explosions, each occurring in the heart of the city between 23:02 and 23:07. Repercussions inevitably ensued, ranging from rioting in the inner city to a cross-country chase for those responsible.

No fewer than twenty people had been confirmed injured.

The terrorists had first been witnessed outside the Scottish Parliament Building after successfully carrying out an apparent heist on the vaults beneath the Royal Mile. Within two hours of their leaving the city, intelligence sources confirmed the culprits were heading north. On reaching the coast, they ran into their biggest challenge.

The mission ended in chaos.

Exactly what the terrorists' motive was remained unclear. The two that had been caught were both French and armed with weapons that usually only showed up on the black market. Both carried artwork, the majority oil on canvas and dating from the 17th century. Also amongst their possessions were manuscripts from the same period of history. Both of the terrorists were known to Interpol.

Both were now behind bars.

The fate of their accomplices remained unknown.

Suffolk, England
01:03, Wednesday 21 March

The black BMW moved swiftly along the tree-lined country roads of Charlestown. The streets were deserted, as they usually were at night. Even in the height of summer, it had never been the liveliest of areas.

The village was smaller than most. The 1,100-strong population recorded at the previous census had further reduced since then, a number meeting their end overseas. Throughout its history, the village had been no stranger to war. From the days that preceded the Domesday Book to the defeat of the Spanish Armada, there was something about it that made it a magnet for soldiers. Most of the villagers had served their country during the darkest days. Those who hadn't had grown up listening to the tales.

The man behind the wheel of the BMW had heard them all before, cherished them even. Many of them held a personal connection, as they concerned the lives of his kin. If someone had witnessed his headlights along the historic high street or light up the nearby side roads where the signposts pointed to farms and hamlets, it would not have aroused suspicion. Even had they not been one of his relatives, they would have been part of the same circle.

Everyone in the village belonged to the same circle.

A second car was in front of him, its full-beamed headlights moving left to right as the driver negotiated the perpetually winding stretch of road. The occupant of the BMW smiled to himself, sound in the knowledge they were unlikely to run into additional traffic. The village didn't appear on the average map. Only a handful of people alive were familiar with the route: a series of unclassified roads that could only be found by those who were either completely lost or knew exactly where they were going. Fewer still drove a black Honda Civic that growled like a Jaguar on steroids when changing gear. His smile widened as the leader of the two-car convoy braked hard, taking up the wrong side of the road as though initiating a drag race. Nothing was at stake but personal pride. If the sounds had been overheard by one of the well-known residents, the response would have been the same. A casual shrug, perhaps a smile.

Even before the invention of the motorcar, the village had been famous for its camaraderie.

As the cars took an apparently innocuous right turn onto an unclassified road, now over three-quarters of a mile from the high street, sights that a tourist could easily mistake as part of an access road to a local farm soon took on a totally different appearance. As the tarmac disappeared, the gravel surface that replaced it continued to an isolated building in over two acres of greenery. What on first impression appeared to be an unused barn, on closer inspection, was something very different. A sign swinging from a freestanding pole alongside the building read simply:

The White Hart Inn.

The BMW skidded to a halt alongside the Honda in one of thirty unused parking bays. The driver took in the sights as he heard the engine tick slowly silent. No lights were shining in the windows of the nearby building, not that he would have expected otherwise. Even in the middle of a city, pubs were rarely found open after midnight on a Tuesday. Nor would there be any great light aiding them from above. Despite the clear star-filled sky, there was no moon; instead, the cloudless darkness and penetrating coldness promised imminent frost. A stranger passing by might have questioned why two such men would be arriving at such a time.

The locals already knew the answer.

As the driver of the BMW got out from behind the wheel, the lights on all sides flashing quickly as he locked the car, he met the driver of the Honda. Despite the lack of light, he could make out the man's features and clothing clearly: a dark blue windproof jacket tailored to his firm physique, almost certainly hiding a USP45 semi-automatic pistol, a PP-19 submachine gun, a special crossbow, and other fancy equipment that he, too, had concealed within his own identical attire. Unlike the last time he saw him, the classic ops suit, operative gloves, combat boots and high-frequency night-vision goggles had been replaced by something more casual. In keeping with his own appearance, his well-toned arms and short, neatly cut hair told a story of a man who had known only one way of life. An amused smile had formed on his lips that appeared slightly raw and chapped after twenty-four hours in the cold of Scotland. Allegedly preceded by three days of non-stop kissing with his fiancée.

"What's this? No gun. You know what they say about taking chances, Mike?" the driver of the Honda said.

The driver of the BMW smiled. "Didn't anyone ever tell you, Kit? Real men make their own luck."

Mike stopped within a few feet of him, arms folded. Their appearances were deceptively similar from a distance, but up close, differences were readily apparent. Kit was in his early thirties, his features still bearing the suppleness of youth, yet with deep green eyes that revealed an air of authority born of experience. Mike's features were somewhat softer, carrying the experience of four years fewer. His eyes displayed clear confidence, a well-defined blue with a mysterious teasing quality.

His friend's name was Kit Masterson.

His, Michael Hansen.

"Besides," Mike continued. "After the night we've had, I could do with something to keep out the cold."

Leaving the cars, the two dark-haired men walked briskly through the unlit car park and stopped at the main entrance. The pub was locked, the lights still extinguished, the sounds of silence interrupted solely by a steady breeze moving through the trees. Visually, the building was easy on the eye. Like the nearby village, its origins dated back to the Middle Ages, with additions to the original half-timbered structure made following damage during the Blitz. Whether accidental or a deliberate attack, the facts of history had never been made known.

Only if it had been deliberate the reasons for the attack would have been self-explanatory.

The Bordeaux Connection

On reaching the door, Mike looked at Kit. "Would you care to do the honours?"

Kit fished a set of keys out of his jeans, unlocked the door and entered. Once inside, he locked it again, and all evidence of their entry vanished. Taking the chance of switching on a light was something that neither of them would have considered. The instruction came from the top.

Not that it was necessary.

As their eyes adjusted to the new surroundings, they walked across the wooden floor. Seeing the pub for the first time, a newcomer would have found the decorations un-noteworthy. The oak-panelled surrounds were largely original, matching a series of round and square tables and chairs that would have been occupied only a few hours earlier by boisterous villagers. During opening hours, the large horseshoe-shaped bar would serve a wealth of ales and lagers from the local counties. Away from the bar, the furnishings were more spartan, as if the lure of a good drink was enticing enough for the townsfolk without needing any extra embellishment. It served a purpose. The village had never been one for outsiders. Should a newcomer arrive, be it a businessman on a journey break, a tourist, or a pilgrim on the wrong trail ignorant of the village's true past, the façade of polite courtesy would always mask a hard inner distrust. If anyone should come with more sinister motives, the same rules applied.

Secrecy could only be maintained without arousing suspicion.

As the two dark-haired men found their way to the opposite side of the counter, they came to a hidden doorway from which a set of twelve wooden steps led down into further darkness. On reaching the bottom, the light changed: a surreal glow emanated from one of the walls, apparently every colour of the spectrum. It was a sight they had seen before; Kit many times, Mike much less. Its source, once upon a time, both had been at a loss to explain. A seemingly permanent wall supporting the building above, its red bricks stained by dirt and cobwebs and partially hidden behind an array of beer kegs, concealed a great secret. On reaching where the light appeared to be coming from, Kit removed a small rectangular key card from his pocket and swiped it, seemingly in mid-air. Over the coming seconds, he heard a series of bleeps, then a short, single one. Finally, a louder sound.

That of the wall moving.

The stonework opened, revealing a second, larger room, visually unlike any either of them had witnessed outside the movie theatre. Its appearance also differed from anything else in the village, reminiscent instead of both a top-secret military bunker and a hi-tech laboratory. A long, single table-like command console occupied the right side of the room. At its centre was a high-speed iMac computer, whose images appeared to float against the far wall like a 3D hologram. Similar electronic equipment flanked the walls, ranging from radar monitoring equipment to landline telephones. While Mike was still to see them in use, their importance was self-evident. Their presence was integral to the organisation's existence and its operations, which were planned and orchestrated around the room's final feature.

At the centre of the room was a large circular oak wood table surrounded by thirteen chairs. A large emblem crossed the table's surface, its features vividly defined. Although the table itself was modern, those familiar with the organisation, and many generations before them, had known numerous predecessors. The emblem had never changed, even since the beginning. The creature was four-legged, solid and magnificent, with two bright eyes looking right of centre, seemingly capable of piercing into the heart of an observer. Unlike the similar sign that adorned the pub, the creature was seated, its facial expression otherwise retiring and docile. Where two mighty antlers stood out on both sides of its head, the image became slightly bizarre. Unlike the white antlers of real life, created by DNA, these were gold and formed of the same material. A similar colour filled the object that hung regally around its neck.

A crown.

The Bordeaux Connection

So completed the image. What an outsider could easily assume to be a typical heraldic image of a forest animal used on a coat of arms of a family of ancient prestige was, in this case, something rather more significant. The creature was white as it always was, after which the order was named. Over the years, they had known many names but only one original.

This was the headquarters of the White Hart, an order founded by royalty and created to operate in secrecy.

Mike and Kit stopped on reaching the table and stood formally to attention. Twelve identical seats surrounded the table, all of the military style, appealing to the eye but designed for business instead of comfort. While the twelve remained vacant, a thirteenth was in use. The man was in his late sixties, his silver hair styled in the same military buzz cut that had been brown forty years earlier. Like the two men before him, he was clean-shaven, his dark suit credible for any officer or politician of high rank and status. His name was immaterial; if he had a real one, Mike had never heard it. He was simply the Director, the spokesman, the King.

They called him Mr White.

"The Prime Minister is due to put out a statement at 07:00 hours tomorrow. Downing Street received the draft less than one hour ago; on this occasion, I decided to prepare it personally. The reasons for this latest endeavour must never be made known. For us, you might say, business as usual. As far as the press is concerned, the business in Edinburgh was merely a botched art theft by members of the criminal underworld, which was misinterpreted as a terrorist attack."

Mike nodded, while beside him, Kit remained quiet and unmoved. The Edinburgh saga had been completely unexpected. A series of explosions on the Royal Mile had been quelled. On this occasion, the heroes of the hour were the local police – at least in the eyes of the media. As far as the wider world was concerned, the White Hart didn't exist; no records were found in government departments, no list of active personnel – past or present. The budget was restricted to 'Black Budget' from the armed forces, just as it had been throughout living memory. An auditor or accountant perusing the relevant files in the main MoD building in London would find only four letters: CNMA. These letters failed to explain their true importance. They stood for Cromwell's New Model Army in honour of the man who had resurrected them from the dead. Less than eighteen months as part of the order, Mike was still to learn every detail. He understood only when not to ask questions. It was a world where the consequences of ego could be destructive. One where the real heroes could never be known. Nor, at least, would they ever be tried in a law court. They were answerable only to one.

Mr White continued, "The PM asked me to pass on his personal thanks to the men in question for their role in helping to avert a national catastrophe."

Kit smiled wryly, silently replaying the recent incident where an overweight Frenchman with links to the criminal underworld had been uncovered holding a portrait of Bonnie Prince Charlie stolen from beneath the National Library. The picture had been recovered, and the enemy arrested.

"Tell him anytime."

Mike's attention became drawn to the empty seats.

"Where are the others?"

"Tonight, there will be no others." The Director rose to his feet and turned towards the control console, entering something into the holographic screen via a slick nine-inch electronic tablet. "The situation in Scotland is over; the mopping up can be left to the local police and, once the two thugs are deported, the *gendarmerie*. It's what they're there for. The other two, for now, remain at large."

Kit bit his lip. "Presumably, they're still in Scotland?"

"Sadly, no. Both were seen leaving Peterhead harbour at 21:21. Searches are being made to locate the boat, but so far, they have come up with nothing. Needless to say, someone's arse is in for a kicking. Several eyewitnesses were able to identify the boat;

whatever it was, it was not native to the harbour or Scotland. As far as I'm aware, no one has been able to track them."

"How about the guards at Edinburgh?"

"Two KIA. The others, so it would seem, had been knocked out by some form of sleeping gas. Fortunately, they were left alone after that."

Mike remained silent. He sensed that the reason for their being summoned so late was not of relevance to the mission. The pictures on the hologram changed to form a large map centred on an area of England, apparently a village or small dwelling in Somerset. A name appeared in bold white lettering.

Montacute.

Mr White turned away from the console, focusing on Mike and Kit. "Take a seat, gentlemen."

Mike eased himself into his usual seat, alongside Kit and with a clear view of the screen. Its pictures changed rapidly, as if software was constantly updating its features. The semi-translucent form was still expanding, the map now a satellite view of the area in question. The pictures sharpened: greenery, trees, and water features all within the grounds of a large estate, at the heart of which was a period mansion.

"What you see before you is Montacute House, a late Elizabethan mansion located in the village of the same name in the south of Somerset. For many years it was owned by the Phelips family before ownership passed to the National Trust. A few days ago, it was the setting of a high-profile gathering hosted by the Duchess of Cornwall."

The pictures changed again. Replacing the satellite overview, Mike saw photographs of a lavish banquet set in the gardens against the picturesque backdrop of well-maintained lawns and woodland. He recognised faces: royals, MPs, and celebrities of slight to moderate fame, from the well respected to the talentless. One face reappeared three times in a row, an actress and former page-three girl Mike had once had a crush on.

"You know, she actually looks better with her clothes on," Kit said.

Mike smiled while Mr White paused the slideshow on a group photograph. He recognised the Prime Minister, the Deputy Prime Minister, two other members of the Cabinet, and their respective partners. All the men were visually familiar.

The women, apart from the PM's wife, less so.

Mr White zoomed in on a blonde-haired woman aged in her early to mid-fifties. She wore a lime green dress and modest earrings and smiled awkwardly. Like most women present, she was attractive.

Mike knew Kit would have had a name for her.

"Do either of you recognise this woman?"

Kit shook his head. "She's not another Lewinsky, is she?"

"Her name is Lavinia Martina Brown or Mrs Christopher Hughes since her marriage. Also, Lady Hughes-Brown since the death of her father," Mr White said, the sound of his fingers tapping against the tablet coinciding with further changes to the screen. "Made her name in the 1980s as a socialite on the Covent Garden scene. These days she's famous for a different reason."

Mike recognised her. "Isn't she married to the Deputy PM?"

"Absolutely correct. Elder sister of the wife of the Earl of Stamford. Favourite of her late father. Eldest of three. During the war, her father had been a Red Beret." He gestured to Mike. "Her mother, on the other hand, had been born in Poland. During the war, many suspected her of being in league with the Kremlin."

"Was she?" Kit asked.

"Only if you believe the tabloids, though she certainly fitted the profile. Poles caught on the wrong side of the country at that time were usually the type the KGB went for. MI6, I'm sure, kept a close watch over her, but nothing was ever proven. She died at the height of the Cold War, so any misdoings she was guilty of slipped the net."

Mike listened whilst simultaneously taking in the woman's features. The latest image to appear was a profile shot, taken not on the day of the party but a head and shoulders view, most likely from a passport or a driving licence. Her hair colour appeared more natural, and her earrings were pearl, with evidence of possible Botox around her chin and neck. Judged on her face alone, she could have passed for early forties.

"Who is she?" Mike asked. "What's so important?"

Mr White walked over to the console and returned carrying what appeared to be a heavy hardback tome. He slid it across the circular table.

"I wonder if this means anything to either of you?"

Kit reached for it before Mike had a chance and examined the cover and the contents. "Can't say that it does, sir. Then again, I've always been more into comic books."

He passed it to Mike, who spent several seconds staring at the frontispiece. The content was paper, over one hundred pages long and library bound. Three things stood out from the start: the author's name, the work's title, and the year of publication.

Sir Walter Raleigh. *The Ocean to Cynthia.* 1599.

Mr White folded his arms. "This mean anything to you, Hansen?"

"Not really, sir. I've never really been much into poetry."

Kit was confused. "I thought Raleigh was a sailor. An adventurer. Hey-ho over the wild blue yonder. Discovering cigarettes and tatties."

"He was," Mike said. "However, he was also a diplomat, a privateer and a poet." He glanced again at the title, recalling something. "Now that you mention it, I thought *The Ocean to Cynthia* had always been described as a lost work."

Mr White's expression changed. "Precisely. In fact, the only copy had been kept at Montacute, along with a famous portrait on loan from the National Portrait Gallery. The book had been kept in the library, owned by the original family for generations. Most scholars would give a spare limb just to touch it."

Kit asked, "What's so special?"

"The book is extremely valuable; however, there is one problem with the version you have." He walked towards Mike, picked up the book and threw it across the floor.

Mike and Kit looked on, dumbstruck. Incredibly, the pages somehow remained intact.

"This version is a fake."

Mike was confused. The appearance of the library-bound cover was exactly as he would have expected, the pages susceptible to signs of wear. There were marks along the seam, which suggested evidence of finger contamination.

"How did you know?"

Mr White turned to face the screen, entered something into his tablet and wandered across the room. The pictures changed again, the large 3D map intercepted in the centre by CCTV footage. The camera was placed in a library and centred on one row of bookshelves. A woman had entered, her blonde hair evident despite the black-and-white pictures.

Judging by her actions, she had no idea she was being filmed.

Mike leaned forward, sensing he knew what was coming. The woman approached the bottom shelf of one of the room's many bookcases, clearly determined not to get dust on her dress. She removed a specific book, placed it carefully inside her surprisingly large designer handbag and replaced it with another.

As far as could be seen from the footage, the covers of both were identical.

Mike was in a daze, Kit even more so. The last twenty-four hours had been hectic: London to Edinburgh, Edinburgh to the wilds of Scotland, the wilds of Scotland to Suffolk.

Neither of them had slept for almost forty-eight hours.

Kit broke the silence. "You brought us here tonight because of a book?"

Mike was thinking the same thing. "If the footage is complete, and assuming she doesn't have any sort of diplomatic immunity, the owner of the house has all the proof they need to press charges. I'm assuming the police are aware of this?"

The Bordeaux Connection

Mr White tapped at his tablet, and the footage on the screen disappeared, along with the maps. A series of photographs took their place, seven in total. The first five were like the ones they'd already seen: group shots of the woman, her husband and several others present at the party, including more of the Prime Minister. The sixth shot was noticeably different. The woman was dressed in darker clothes, a black leather jacket and stockings. A black fedora hat hid most of her hair and face; even in the still frames, it was apparent her movements were stifled. Mike recognised the location: Tower Bridge.

Then: Westminster.

The photos changed again. The latest had been taken at King's Cross Station; the woman was standing on one of the platforms. She was talking to someone, a man: late thirties, dark hair, somewhere between five-ten and six feet tall. They recognised him immediately.

They had seen him earlier that night.

In Scotland.

Mike and Kit watched as Mr White doubled the size of the final two photographs. In them, the Deputy Prime Minister's wife passed over the book she had taken from the stately home. She proceeded to leave the platform while the recipient boarded the train.

The sign on the platform confirmed the train was heading to Edinburgh.

Kit looked back, arms folded. "I'm guessing this can't be a coincidence."

Mr White raised his eyebrows. "The man's name is Fabien Randek. Born and raised in Marseille, served three years in the French Foreign Legion before going missing in Tangiers. Re-emerged back in his hometown two years later and was arrested on suspicion of drug trafficking. Nothing was found; of course, you know all this."

Kit nodded, his trademark half-smile forming. Mike also knew the name. Everyone who sat at that table knew the basic story. The

White Hart demanded only one thing of every operative: perfection, including instant knowledge. The man was ranked a red star, the second highest rank in the order's danger category. Most of their backgrounds ranged from terrorism and military to drug trafficking, theft and arson. Purple was the highest, green the lowest.

"Until tonight, I'd honestly thought that SOB had disappeared down a ditch somewhere. Where the hell's he been hiding?" Kit asked.

"Disappeared, yes. Where he's been exactly, who knows? Sources in Marseille have been quiet ever since his older brother was killed two years ago when Interpol raided an apartment block in his old estate. A couple of weeks ago, he turned up in Bordeaux. Renting a four-by-four of all things."

"What's the latest intel?" Mike asked. "I'm guessing he must have a good reason for letting off bombs north of the border?"

Mr White's expression remained non-committal. "The garden party took place on Saturday – two days before the explosions on the Royal Mile. The meeting at King's Cross was on the Sunday, the eighteenth. If there is a connection, the theft of the Raleigh book might have been the first in the chain."

Kit was intrigued. The theft seemed uninteresting compared to what could have been taken. "Are you sure he got away tonight?"

"Did you kill him?" Mike asked.

"No. I always remember a face. If the bastard's dead, it wasn't me who shot him."

"Trust me, neither of you did. He's still alive and currently on a boat somewhere, most likely in the North Sea. As far as I'm aware, no one died, apart from the two guards already mentioned. The two Frenchmen you captured have both been identified. One had recently been upgraded to amber; the other wasn't listed at all. Whatever Randek's involvement in this, I think we can safely assume he's a long way above being a footman. Area management would be my guess."

"So, not the boss?" Mike asked.

The Bordeaux Connection

"You think a boss would collect something in person on a train platform in broad daylight in London from a politician's wife?" Kit asked.

Mike grimaced, too late to withdraw the question. "How about any known history involving antiquities or art? Ownership, theft, employment – that sort of thing? The thugs we captured had a bag full of art and literature."

"If you dig deep enough, you'll find his background covers most areas. His uncle once worked as a courier for a man named Victor Varane. Before your time. One of the key players in the Marseille underworld – all very French Connection."

"How about resale?" Kit interjected. "Maybe he's just a thief or a middleman."

Mike shook his head. "If so, most likely, he already has a buyer lined up, or he's simply taken the attack as an opportunity to fill his bag. Either that or he intends to use something as collateral for a drug shipment or a loan."

"Be that as it may," Mr White replied, silently impressed by the talents of his men, "our job is not of concern with the theft at Montacute itself. As you rightly say, theft of property is a police matter; the CCTV footage already confirms the guilt.

"Our problem lies in the why and who. A woman of Mrs Hughes's reputation seen gallivanting across London with stolen property, taken whilst she was a guest at a formal occasion in the company of the PM and her husband, can only be good news for the tabloids and the leader of the opposition. Not that this getting out would necessarily be in his best interests. Furthermore, the fact that Randek was involved tonight makes the situation all the more complicated."

Kit stared contemplatively. "You think she's a party to terrorism?"

"Whether she is or isn't, there's enough evidence here to put her away for several years. Of greater concern to the PM is the deputy."

Mike was shocked. "You mean he suspects the Deputy PM was involved in last night's attacks?"

Mr White's expression became distant. "For over twenty years, Mrs Hughes has been well known in London high society; even today, she isn't completely unknown to Fleet Street. That said, since the last election and the surprise rise of her husband in the coalition government, it's fair to say she's learned to curb her enthusiasm. Her link with Randek might be unknown to her husband. After all, it wouldn't be the first time a politician has been compromised by a family member. That said, there might be more in it."

Kit was struggling with the possibility. "Even if he was involved, I hardly see the DPM as the type who would sell out his own country. I mean, I know he's Eton."

Mike smiled, aware that the college had a chequered history with double agents. "I suppose the real question is, what's her business with Randek? Are the two well acquainted, or was this set up through a go-between?"

"Answers to this and more will surely come to light when the lady is questioned. But we digress. The involvement of Randek, though unwelcome, might, in fact, be a blessing in disguise. Scotland Yard and Interpol blazing in kicking and screaming might succeed in catching book and art thieves. However, if done properly, she might serve better in other ways. So far, the vermin picked up in Peterhead have failed to offer any revealing insights."

Mike raised an eyebrow. "You mean you want us to use her as bait?"

"No, you imbecile," Kit said, "he means the PM wants us to use her as bait."

Mr White threw Kit a stern expression. "As you well know, I don't believe in coincidences. I've been in this job far too long. Any prior knowledge of the DPM to the theft could have far-reaching repercussions. At best, tabloid fodder; at worst, involvement with some of the most wanted men on the continent."

The Bordeaux Connection

Mike listened attentively. Despite feeling the effects of over forty-eight hours without proper sleep, his mind had entered overdrive. "What did you have in mind? Question the DPM or simply follow him?"

"Parliament is sitting tomorrow to discuss the actions of the last two days – saving our involvement, of course. Mr Hughes's office is in the Cabinet Office, a pokey little place on the first floor. His London residence is also in Whitehall, an apartment adjoining the Old Admiralty Building. The woman herself has an apartment in Knightsbridge once owned by her father that she apparently still uses from time to time."

"You don't mean to say she's presently at large?" Kit asked.

"No, staying with her husband at Dorneywood. It's been the main country home since the election. It's the same place Prescott was photographed playing croquet on the lawn. Being the Deputy PM, Mr Hughes doesn't have a set weekend place. In fact, the PM makes him share Dorneywood with the Chancellor and Chevening with the Foreign Secretary."

"I take it then Mr Hughes is the only minister under suspicion?" Mike asked, quietly concentrating on the way Mr White paused before answering. The man was living up to his reputation: cold, hard, and pragmatic, but not without a personality thriving in panache.

Kit realised Mike had a point. "There were a number of them there in Somerset."

"In my experience, cases like these are the most awkward. When working in the Cabinet, the assumption of trust should always be paramount. Even in the Third World, harmonious cooperation can frequently demonstrate successful policy. Yet, even in our green and pleasant land, governments have been known to fall apart when colleagues and friends of twenty years have suddenly fallen out for one reason or another."

Mike asked, "If the PM is so worried about the trust of his allies, why doesn't he just ask the CID to perform an enquiry? I'm guessing GCHQ are already listening to their calls."

Mr White laughed. "Why not call in *The Times* and the *Express*? The PM is understandably worried any leaks might severely hurt the election campaign. Not to mention the harm it would do to our attempts to answer any real questions.

"The matter of the missing book aside, the case before us has the potential to be of mutual interest. If the DPM, his wife, or any other members of the Cabinet are involved with any known terrorist organisation, or any other members of the criminal underworld, this could be the key to unlocking the door."

"Not to mention, end their careers and put them away for a long time," Mike said.

"As I put to you when you arrived here, Hansen. What's the greatest crime? The crime that occurred yesterday or the crime that occurs tomorrow?"

"How exactly do you propose we go about this?" Kit asked, interrupting. "I'm sure the DPM won't take too kindly to being shadowed by nameless operatives. Worse, he'll probably assume we're members of the press. Either that or MI5."

"Not to mention what the rest of Westminster might think of two such good-looking newcomers," Mike added.

"I'm not suggesting you address him in public. The opposite, in fact." The Director removed a set of keys from his pocket and threw them across the table. "The PM is most insistent you carry this out with minimum fuss. The Commons, as mentioned, is scheduled to sit, most likely before ten. The DPM's office will be vacant, not to mention his government residence and country ones. I suggest you put the time to good use."

Kit failed to hide a smile. He hadn't misheard. The Prime Minister of the UK had personally handed over keys to the important chambers of his deputy.

"And his wife?" Mike asked.

"I want no stone left unturned; I've already made arrangements for Dorneywood and the flat in Knightsbridge. That leaves only the office at Number 70 and the apartment in Admiralty House. Find out everything there is to know about their activities, from their recent contacts book to what underwear they've been wearing. Any links to Randek will be sufficient for the CID – not to mention all their European equivalents. And for us, maybe some answers as to what really caused whatever the hell happened in Edinburgh."

Mike and Kit were gone within moments. Any evidence that a secret briefing had taken place in the pub's cellar quickly vanished. The two cars left the car park and headed along the unclassified road back into the heart of the village. A third, parked out of sight in a nearby garage, would remain where it was, its owner's route home instead involving a short walk up the flight of stairs and into the lodgings of the landlord.

Mike followed Kit midway along the high street and into a secluded courtyard where twelve Tudor houses had been constructed to form the perfect circle. On stopping the car, Mike examined the keys closely for the first time. There were ten in all, each for the locks of important doors connected to the Cabinet Office. There would be no room for error. Entry into the office of a cabinet minister was the stuff of spy thrillers, even in a nation where black ops were widely accepted as reasonable and necessary. Even compared to other high-risk assignments, the margins for this one were tight.

Any mistakes and the headlines on the front pages could be worse than if the PM's fears were correct.

London
09:11, Wednesday 21 March

The two suited men emerged from the train at Westminster Tube station and joined the ever-growing flow of passengers heading out onto the concourse. Their appearances were eye catching, but not out of character for the area. It was a part of the world where most people were smartly dressed, where politicians and bankers walked the streets in unison, along with other individuals of equal importance.

Being after 09:00, the peak period of activity had passed, but the station at Westminster was rarely deserted. On summer days, it was a spot to which tourists from all over the world would flock. Large cameras and lenses hung around their necks and their index fingers snapped away, taking souvenir shots of the Houses of Parliament and the nearby landmarks. The Commons, in particular, had been in the news constantly of late. The reports from Edinburgh dominated most front pages, rumour abounding of possible future attacks.

Rumour spread fast in London. A word from a so-called expert tended to be accepted as a fundamental truth by many in the city. There was an atmosphere in the air: impatience but also uncertainty. Steady queues formed at the ticket office by Portcullis House, where eager tourists attempted to obtain tickets for guided tours of Parliament. Others tried to gain access to the viewing gallery on what would potentially be a historic day for the Commons. Those who weren't in town to work were there to observe a moment of escape from the mundane. It was a pattern that repeated itself. The only things that changed were the names of the key players.

And even they were usually forgotten within a week.

The Bordeaux Connection

The two smartly dressed men emerged from the main stairway and stopped on reaching the street. They took a moment to check their surroundings before heading speedily toward the Houses of Parliament.

Kit took the lead. He looked at his watch as they passed Westminster Abbey, the great east façade of which towered over them. Further along the street, he stopped again, comparing his watch with Big Ben.

After six years on the job, things came naturally to him. A hot dog stand or a man with a briefcase waiting patiently on the side of the road was a common occurrence in almost any city in the world. Still, it was also in such places that outsiders often sought to blend into their surroundings without arousing suspicion. Tourists moving quickly in and out of the crowds, suited men chatting to one another or to unseen callers on their mobile phones were likely to be an innocent sight 99.99 per cent of the time.

He was paid to worry about that 0.01 per cent.

Mike walked quickly to Kit's right, his hands swinging side to side. They would have taken a car in a different location, but that was never a good idea in London. Even in the inner city, a well-thought-out operation with hours of planning could still go down the drain because of a traffic jam, a fatal accident, or a cyclist in the wrong place at the wrong time. The streets around Westminster had already reached gridlock. Horns honked, engines revved, and drivers waited impatiently for the traffic to clear and the lights to turn green.

Kit checked his watch for the second time in a minute. "We've got about twenty-seven minutes till we begin. Parliament is scheduled for a nine thirty start. Ordinarily, that would give us at least an hour till the flock leaves the field. If we're lucky, today might be a long one."

Mike nodded, matching Kit step for step. He'd visited Westminster countless times, both as a tourist and on the job, but today he sensed extra energy in the air. The PM had spoken on the air less than twenty-four hours earlier; apparently, he'd done so again that morning. The seriousness of the situation was clear; the press weren't the only people gunning for answers.

In all likelihood, Mike guessed it would be a long day for the MPs.

"Are you quite sure you're happy to go ahead with this?" Kit asked, his usual smile forming. "Ten minutes should be enough, and I can join you."

Mike grinned. "You just worry about your thing. You can buy me a hot dog when it's over."

Inside the House of Commons, the Prime Minister shook his head in resigned irritation as the leader of the opposition launched a trademark tirade on the coalition for their lack of direction. People on both sides of the house oohed and aahed: the classic sounds of the Commons. The older members had seen it all before. Five years since the last election, a hung parliament that initially pleased no one, had seen relative progress and a country united by a common purpose.

Yet today was an exception. News of the latest terror threat from north of the border, accompanied by tabloid rumours of further planned raids on other major UK cities, had a familiar ring. The older generation remembered the IRA days with morbid fascination. All could recount how even the slightest movement among the undercroft could mean anything from an insect to an incendiary. The latest account had more in keeping with its recent troubles: spies and saboteurs mixed with stories of criminal syndicates that seemed right out of a Ross Kemp documentary.

The only thing missing was a reference to Islamic extremism.

Sitting alongside the PM, the Deputy PM leaned to his right and whispered to the man alongside him. While the Deputy PM was bearded, his once athletic physique weighed down by a few extra pounds, his hair a distinguished silver, alongside him, the wiry, clean-shaven bald man was less handsome. As Foreign Secretary, he'd been second on the line to Edinburgh after the Home Secretary. The purple shade of his eyelids confirmed sleep in recent days had been rare. The process had opened with him, a speech that lasted less than five minutes but as direct in purpose as the majority of Members had heard from him. Two of the culprits had been arrested and would be deported after questioning.

Only two remained at large.

Away from the highly charged atmosphere of the Commons, two men of military pedigree were preparing to enter two very different luxury abodes.

In many ways, the rural setting of the first had made the blond man's job easier. The residents were no strangers to wealth. A brand new 4x4 moving steadily along one of the muddy country roads, the driver's face hidden by tinted glass, was typical of day-to-day life.

Despite the house's famed importance, the security left a lot to be desired. After avoiding the main gate, the journey across the well-manicured grounds had proven equally straightforward. The suggestion had come from the best possible source. With the current tenants in Westminster, observation was less likely. The estate formed the heart of the local countryside: 215 acres of sprawling woodland and parkland, including rose garden displays that brought in tourists on days of invitation.

Even from a distance, the house was clearly visible. The view from the back was like that of the front: the reddish/brown brick walls and darker roof in keeping with the original Georgian façade that was partially plagued by moss. The main house was surrounded by a series of outer buildings, the majority of which he understood were currently used in the day-to-day running of the estate.

Staying close to the trees, which shielded him from both the wind and possible observation, the intruder made his way towards the rear of the mansion.

The next step would depend purely on timing.

The task awaiting the second man was altogether different. His dark hair and polished appearance was in keeping with most who occupied the building. Even during the day, Knightsbridge was rarely deserted. To a passer-by taking the stairs or the lift, brief acknowledgements of a polite smile or a casual "Good morning" were unlikely to arouse much suspicion. Aside from issuing him a timely reminder that sometimes the worst place to get lost is in a crowd.

Research confirmed property in these parts rarely came up for sale. On the top floor, the residents kept themselves to themselves, even if their identities were known to one another. It was a constant factor, something the building epitomised. Only one of a certain class was welcome.

And class often attracted attention.

The building's appearance was identical to the others in the street. From the top of the road, the white Georgian crescent looked like something out of a Jane Austen novel. Despite the relatively late hour, most of the parking spaces were in use, their number plates and brands appropriate to the local profile. It was cool, despite the sunlight; a steady breeze blew across Hyde Park, bracing against the faces of those strolling the main pathways.

The dark-haired man had waited patiently. It wasn't the type of place to break into in the middle of the day, even with the correct keys. The Director had mentioned that the fire escape, a subtle albeit very metallic structure that most residents viewed as an eyesore, was located at the rear of the building. Taking the tour of the street, he headed back towards the park and then changed direction on reaching the corner of the crescent.

If his intel was correct, the woman would be home within the hour.

The Cabinet Office
09:30

The man whose face was among the least recognisable in Whitehall stood alone in a deserted office in Number 70. Entry had been surprisingly easy.

He had the Deputy PM's boss to thank for that.

The building was quieter than usual. Though the ministers were absent, the majority sprawled out across the famous green padded seats of the Commons, watching proceedings with varying degrees of interest, it was business as usual for the staff. Smartly dressed individuals regularly walked up and down the Victorian corridors, papers and briefcases in hand, the background buzz of numerous conversations coming through the open doorways. Despite the historic décor and timeless furniture, white walls showcasing fine examples of the government's vast art collection, the manner of the organisation was unmistakably modern. The formerly genteel, slow-paced ambience of the early Commonwealth era had been replaced by Bluetooth phones, HD computer systems, portable tablets and faces of every age and race. While the surroundings characterised much of what the wider world stereotyped as British, Kit detected a hint of Europe amongst the background noises: staff welcoming visiting diplomats. He had been prepared for one of the MPs to pass him along one of the corridors. The Home Secretary strutting the halls as if fresh from an hour in the salon or the chief whip stinking of brandy. He remembered his first visit to the building; he'd come in through the front door and among a party of twelve.

Today could not have been more different.

When Mr White first highlighted the enormity of the task, the first question that came to mind was about access.

Kit's appearance was perfect. In keeping with those who regularly occupied the building, it blended the impeccably smart and the uniform. Rule number one of espionage: attract no attention – even an idiot knew that. The politicians aside, it was the principal place of employment for most of the 2,000-strong staff that made up the Cabinet Office. Walking a busy set of corridors, dressed in a smart suit, a security tag dangling from below his left breast, he was unlikely to arouse suspicion. Particularly while the politicians were away.

Getting inside, however, was another matter. In recent years, he had heard a rumour of secret passages above and below, but until now, he had never used one.

Nor, until last night, had he ever expected to.

The plan, he now knew, had been watertight. It had been tried and tested many times in missions going back to before World War Two. After separating from Mike at the bottom of Whitehall, rather than using the traditional entry into Number 70 and having his every action witnessed by the suspicious glances of on-duty policemen, he entered a building that was more famous still. Adjacent to the Cabinet Office, 10 Downing Street was busy with daily activities. The PM inevitably was absent due to attending the debate in the Commons.

After being escorted inside by the PM's chief of staff and watching staff cleaning the downstairs from top to bottom, Kit made a journey he never would have believed possible. While the corridor's tiled floor had a modern feel, the red bricks surrounding it were authentic Tudor, and the views through the window iconic. If historical records of the building were correct, he was walking the same passage that had once been used every morning by the man who married six wives. Yet where once a real tennis court had been the destination, today its use was more discreet. Its modern name was the Cockpit Passage.

A secret route into the Cabinet Office enjoyed only by the rulers of England.

The Bordeaux Connection

The final part of the journey had been reassuringly straightforward. Indeed, the walk along the landing was achieved without the need even to make eye contact. While on any other day, he would have made use of one of his strongest assets – his intensely bright and vivid green eyes – today, a smart pair of designer glasses took the place of his usual contact lenses. The mission called for anonymity, to fade into the shadows and recesses of the building, as opposed to charming those around him to help him achieve his objectives.

Even if Sharon didn't kill him, he knew the PM would.

The office of the Deputy PM was both tasteful and practical. An ornate fireplace was set into white walls furnished with original artworks and complemented by antique furniture that had scarcely been moved since the days of the British Empire. A matching set of leather settees and armchairs surrounded a Queen Anne table on which a Victorian tea set had been placed. All were close to a grandfather clock that ticked out its rhythmic tones below a portrait of Admiral Nelson, one of many in the room of nautical prestige.

Ignoring the surroundings, Kit headed for the room's most important feature, close to the main windows. The Deputy PM's desk was surprisingly modern, covered in stationery and illuminated by natural and artificial lighting. The first thing that caught his eye was a red leather-bound box decorated in the centre with the golden insignia of the monarch, famous worldwide as the property of a cabinet minister. Six years in the order had taught him that only one included writing.

That belonging to the Chancellor of the Exchequer.

The computer was switched on, which was a bonus. Kit had heard a rumour in some quarters that the most secure computers in the building were equipped with a trip switch – the latest breakthrough in anti-hacking technology. Moving the mouse to interrupt the screensaver, a window emerged, requiring a password to continue.

Adjusting his jacket, he removed a small electronic device from his inside left pocket, physically identical to a memory stick. He inserted it into the USB drive, again thankful he had not encountered any obstacles. A green light flashed persistently for five seconds before stopping. At the same moment, the screen changed.

He was in.

Kit adjusted his glasses and pulled at his right ear. The second reason for his choice of eyewear had been tactical.

"I'm in."

In the secret room in Suffolk, Mr White stood alongside two people from very different backgrounds. On his right, the senior technician in his early thirties placed his hand on his three-day stubble and tugged at his loose-fitting shirt that was unbuttoned at the collar. On the Director's left, a serious-looking woman with jet-black hair, wearing a brown suit and a similar earpiece to Kit, looked emotionlessly at the central command console.

She heard Kit's voice come through clearly. "Understood. Keep in regular contact." She turned to Mr White. "Edward to White Seven."

Near Kit's location, Mike's journey to the other end of Whitehall had required a more direct approach.

Admiralty House was another of London's significant locations. At one time, the four-storey yellow brick building had been the principal residence of the First Lord of the Admiralty before later serving as a temporary home for the Prime Minister when Number 10 was undergoing renovation. Sited within a quarter of a mile of the Cabinet Office, it was officially Grade I listed and continued to be used exclusively for Government purposes and accommodation.

Mike had moved quickly. After parting from Kit along the A3212, better known as Whitehall, he blended in with the masses as he headed north towards the National Gallery. He ignored any temptation to get side-tracked by the signposts leading to Downing Street or Whitehall Place.

Admiralty House was an impressive sight. Like virtually all buildings in the heart of government, it was only possible to gain access if you knew how. To the building's right, the Old Admiralty Building was equally imposing. Its east side was guarded by a thick stone wall that incorporated Palladian-style pillars and an entrance reminiscent of Marble Arch, decorated with a rooftop parapet and mirroring Pegasus.

The gate was closed: no surprises. Whitehall was bustling. Holidaymakers and office workers made their way with varying degrees of purpose in both directions, the majority heading for either the tourist sights or the Tube. A security guard carried out a lone vigil: a dark-haired man dressed in a luminous jacket; to a casual observer, he could have been an ambulance driver. There was a second smaller gate behind the first pillar left of the entrance. Two more were cut into the wall directly outside Admiralty House, also closed.

Entry from the front would be impossible without the necessary security pass.

To the west of Admiralty House, St James's Park was its usual haven away from the busy city. Tourists walked the main pathways, occasionally stopping to buy fast food before heading north-east towards Charing Cross Tube station or south-west to Buckingham Palace.

East of the park, people walked across Horse Guards Parade. Some stopped to take panoramic shots of the Old Admiralty Building, the Household Cavalry Museum, Scotland Office and the Guards' Memorial, which was a rare treat in the glorious sunshine. Among them, Admiralty House was surrounded by hedging that separated it from the monument of the Ottoman Gun. To the left of Admiralty House, the southern side of the Old Admiralty Building towered regally above the parade ground like an emperor's mansion, its red and orange colours warmly reflecting the morning sun. Scaffolding had been erected across part of both buildings, obscuring the right side of the main façade and the four storeys of the rear of Admiralty House. On a work area of the roof, a group of construction workers dressed in luminous jackets and hard hats was deeply engaged in conversation.

Mike took in the situation from the park before moving on once more. Neither those nearby nor the museum staff noticed him enter the Old Admiralty Building and continue his walk towards the residence of the Deputy Prime Minister.

The Cabinet Office, Whitehall
10:17

The password was Lavinia. Kit recognised the name. Two people in the man's family had been called by that name. His wife and her poodle.

Kit guessed it was after the poodle!

Three minutes had passed, but it seemed like a lot longer. Usually, even ninety seconds was too long; anything beyond five minutes was almost unthinkable. The reports he had got from Maria, the attractive brunette who at one point had made it difficult for him to concentrate on the job, confirmed that the Commons was still in session. While the PM responded at length to various questions from around the house, the DPM was in the same place, chatting intermittently with the PM or the Foreign Secretary.

Kit knew the man was going nowhere for a long time.

He kept a close eye on the door. The area outside was a long narrow corridor with a landing at the top of the stairs. He had saved digital images of the building's blueprints on his mobile phone, taken from documents in the archives. Unlike the computer games that had gotten him through university, no red dots were moving along the corridor, denoting possible enemies. Fortunately, he knew Maria had obtained a satellite link-up.

Despite that, something was bothering him. The soothing sound of classical music was floating through the building; it was unclear from where it came or whether it was a live performance or stereo speakers. Although the rising pitch of the cellos and violins gave him an unexpected lift, the music worried him. Aside from confirming a nearby presence, music could mask other sounds.

Including footsteps.

A quick sweep of the hard drive confirmed the content was a mixed bag. Many of the files were MS Office based. Letters and emails between colleagues and other personnel, email attachments, files related to the man's position and office and other stuff that seemed to belong more on a personal computer. Looking for specific information and details relating to the theft of the Raleigh manuscript or connections to the terror attacks in Edinburgh was like looking for a needle in China.

The only option was to download everything.

He removed a small external hard drive from his pocket, a flat black device shaped like a calculator that connected via a lead to the USB drive.

"I'm downloading the data now; might take a few minutes."

Back at the White Hart Inn, Maria was standing alone by the control console. "Copy that, Edward." When conducting conversations by radio, they always used their codenames. "Commons is still in session; you should be free for another hour."

Assuming no one else comes in, he thought grimly. "You're quite sure he's not the type of chap who leaves his keys lying around?"

"Unlikely," she smiled wryly. "For some reason, MPs are usually uptight about their privacy. Speaking of which, don't forget to check the drawers. You never know what might be hidden there."

Kit couldn't believe she'd suggested something that obvious. As the external hard drive flashed in a consistent pattern, he opened the top drawer on the left side and began sifting through the contents.

The first thing he saw caught his eye. "Concert tickets. Dvořák." He associated the name with the music he was hearing. Clearly, someone else in the near vicinity had the famous composer on their mind.

After several seconds of silence, Maria spoke. "Bohemian Legends. Dvořák's *Rusalka*. Tonight at the Royal Opera House. According to this, it's a sell-out."

The Bordeaux Connection

The information agreed with the words on the ticket. "Apparently, he has box seats. They're dated tonight."

"They would be. According to the venue website, it's the second night of two."

"When was the first?"

"Yesterday. There are reviews in the *Mail* and the *Telegraph*."

Kit decided against asking her how she knew the facts so quickly.

Maria resumed, "Out of interest, where are they seated?"

"Why? You interested?" He checked the tickets. "Grand Tier. Box 63."

A brief pause. "Wow. Just shows how far a little influence can go. Mr Hughes couldn't have picked better seats."

"Let me guess? First row, centre of the middle tier, right next to the director?"

"Not quite. Right of centre. Four boxes along from the Queen."

Kit raised an eyebrow. Thinking it over, he remembered that the more distinguished guests usually had seats close to the stage.

"Is she likely to be attending?"

"Unlikely. The Royal Box is a lot like the one at Wimbledon; it's always there in reserve. I'll make enquiries, though. You never know, maybe a distant relative."

The idea was disturbing. The less the gossip columns had to do with the event, the better.

"What else is there?"

Kit explored the top drawer, finding stationery, CDs, papers and magazines. "Just the usual. Pens, paperclips, notepaper." He returned the tickets and closed the drawers, glancing quickly at the download.

Less than two minutes remained.

He tried the second drawer, then the third, before doing the same with an additional three on the right side of the desk. As he started on the fourth, he picked up the pace. He sensed the music was getting louder; unmistakably, the iconic sounds of a large orchestra were now accompanied by a strong voice singing words in a European language.

"Maria, you're a nice, cultured girl. What does this opera sound like to you?"

"You're not going to sing to me, are you?"

He grinned. "No. I can hear music. I think it's Dvořák. Can you hear it in the background?"

She listened for several seconds while Kit continued to rummage through the drawers. "Not clearly, but you might have a point. Where's it coming from?"

"Not sure. Possibly the floor below. The voice sounds live."

"Wherever it is, it must be on pretty loud."

"My thoughts exactly." Kit started on the last drawer. "Whatever it is, I get the distinct feeling the Deputy PM isn't the only person planning on attending tonight. Is there any chance you could find out?"

"I'll see what comes up. In the meantime, I'll pass on the information to the King." She spoke of the Director of the White Hart. "You get yourself out of there."

Kit closed the drawer and removed the external hard drive from the USB port before returning the computer to its previous state and locking the taskbar.

As he sought to leave, he noticed something.

"Hughes's briefcase is beneath the desk. What say I plant a wire?"

Unbeknown to Kit, Mr White was now alongside her. "Roger that," she said.

Kit picked up the briefcase and carefully examined the exterior. The locks opened with two short clicks. Experience told him the best place to hide a microphone would be under the flap beneath the top of the lining.

He removed a small wire, no larger than a human hair, from his inside pocket and attached it beneath the leather before returning the case to its original position.

"Mission complete. I'm heading out."

The Bordeaux Connection

On the floor below, the cellist ceased his improvised performance and turned off the nearby stereo. Playing always relaxed him, but there was nothing like practising to a musical accompaniment. It made everything seem more real, giving him rushes of adrenaline that could only be achieved by being part of the real thing. He wasn't as familiar with this opera as most, but opera was opera. God's personal method of communication. The language of the angels.

As the music ceased, he walked across the office to the mahogany table and poured himself a cup of tea from the porcelain teapot he had filled five minutes earlier. The nearby clock said it was approaching 10:20. Parliament was unlikely to adjourn for another hour, he thought. Following the events of the previous two days, it would be unlikely to end before twelve.

At which point the minister would arrive.

Taking the first sip of his tea, he opened his leather briefcase and examined the contents. *Beautiful*, he thought. Like the instrument he'd just been playing, the item could only be found in Eastern Europe. The container itself told little of the story, nor was it meant to. It was the liquid inside it that would do the damage. With the appropriate detonation, it would solidify, so he was told; then, once it reached a certain heat, crystallise.

Then KA-BOOM.

He smiled to himself as he closed the briefcase and returned to his cello. With music once again blaring from the stereo speakers, he was oblivious to the sound of footsteps heading along the Cockpit Passage.

Admiralty House, Whitehall
10:20

The apartment wasn't what Mike had expected, not that he had known what to expect. Whereas the images Maria had sent to his phone of the rooms on the ground floor – labelled Music Room, Drawing Room, Dining Room, Entrance Hall – depicted an interior in keeping with its past, the apartment on the second floor was of mixed furnishings and predominantly masculine.

There were no photographs on file of the apartment itself – or at least none since the present tenant had taken up occupancy. Those of the other rooms dated back to before 2010, taken from the White Hart's rich intelligence collection.

He had entered the building via a passageway that led from the Old Admiralty Building into the music room. Bright yellow walls reflected the light of countless table lamps and overhead chandeliers that illuminated a wealth of red antique chairs. A multicoloured rug covered much of the floor while offering further evidence that the government's expansive art collection was still enjoyed by the select few. A statuary marble fireplace occupied one of the walls, with pedestals honouring female marble busts on either side. Several fruit bowls had been placed on top of the wooden furniture; whether real or for show, he was unable to tell.

He avoided the temptation to sample it.

He moved quietly, wary of being seen. Like the other rooms on the ground floor, fortunately, no one was home. On reaching the stairs, he continued upwards to the third floor and entered using the keys provided by Mr White.

Unlike the communal rooms on the ground floor, the private quarters of the Deputy PM gave off an aura of freshness and were awash with colour. Thick leather couches rested on a cream-coloured carpet, partially covered by matching red rugs, one of

The Bordeaux Connection

which seemed strangely afflicted with dog hairs. On the other side of the room was a large wall-mounted, widescreen television that, according to the display, had recently been connected to an external device. On the sideboard was a selection of magazines covering subjects ranging from history to camping. A picture of Goering decorated the front cover of one concerned with history. *Goering*, Mike thought. *Cream-coloured carpets!*

Unlikely in Churchill's day.

The photographs Maria had sent had suggested a closed-plan design, typically Georgian. The apartment, however, was more open than Mike had expected. Once finished with the lounge, he found himself in the kitchen, then a small dining room, before ending with two bedrooms. Most of the furniture came with the property, but there was evidence of recent habitation. A fully stocked fridge that included a recently defrosted toad-in-the-hole and the cluttered wardrobe and chest of drawers indicated the occupant would soon return.

He re-entered the living room, satisfied the kitchen was clear. "Everything looks clear. What am I looking for, Maria?"

A male voice replied. "Phil, actually. Maria's talking to Edward."

A wry smile. "Must be my unlucky day. What are we looking for?"

"The DPM's briefcase was in his office. Edward's already been there. Currently, he's downloading data from the computer. We already have a lead on his next movement."

"Great. What's our best bet here?"

"Any sign of any laptops or androids?"

"Nothing yet," Mike said, scanning the surrounding area. "Plenty of magazines, books, DVDs in a holder. Interestingly the TV source was last set to external. Looks as though it was recently connected to a phone or a tablet."

"Interesting. What else do you see?"

"Not much," Mike said. "Lounge is clear. I'm gonna try the kitchen."

A second sweep of the kitchen came up trumps. A mobile phone was charging on the work surface.

"Found your 'android'! It's actually a brand-new iPhone; fifty per cent battery." He picked it up and attempted to access the desktop. "Access is encrypted: a four-digit code."

"Inside your belt, you should have a small rectangular box. Open it and remove the black-cased item, third from the left. Remove the charger from the phone and insert it into the charger socket."

Mike followed the instructions, inserting the small memory stick into the charger port. The display on the iPhone lit up, following which a series of patterns appeared.

"Phil, it's messing with the content."

"Good. It's meant to. Give it another five seconds."

Mike bit his lip, suddenly nervous. Any damage to the phone would undoubtedly arouse suspicion. He kept his eyes on the screen, the coloured display now a series of black lines moving across a flashing green background. After six solid seconds of erratic behaviour, the display returned to normal.

"It's clear. And I've got access."

"Try to access voicemail. Better yet, the call register."

Again Mike followed directions, navigating the options. "According to this, a call took place last night. Commenced at 22:37 and terminated at exactly 23:00."

"Understood. That might be interesting."

"You think you can trace them?"

"You let me worry about that."

Mike smiled, knowing Phil probably had his ways. The man was a computer nut, the type of person the Americans would have dubbed a geek in college and nicknamed IT in the military. In his own way, the most important person involved.

"No voicemails. Only four texts. All from family. Seems clean."

"When you're ready, plug it back in and leave. Keep me posted."

"Will do."

The Bordeaux Connection

Mike replaced the phone, leaving the kitchen in the same state. He moved through the master bedroom, then the second, ending with a final check of the lounge.

As he approached the front door, he heard footsteps on the landing.

"Phil, I hear footsteps. Is Parliament over?"

"Not likely. If in doubt, leave through one of the lounge windows. Use the scaffolding to get down."

A good idea, he decided. "Roger that. I'm heading out."

The Old Admiralty Building, Whitehall
10:42

The Old Admiralty Building was a labyrinth of corridors, each steeped in history. Winston Churchill had walked them frequently at the height of the war, holding meetings with navy top brass as he sought to mastermind Allied victory in the North Atlantic.

Visually it was a picture. Like the four-storey Admiralty House it adjoined, the historic Georgian structure overlooking Horse Guards Parade had commanded pride of place in the heart of the capital since the Jacobite Rebellion. Officially it was the largest of the so-called Admiralty complex of character buildings located between Downing Street and Admiralty Arch at the tip of the Mall, its total area of 20,000 square metres, a unique combination of historic furniture and modern-day occupants. It didn't look like a military HQ; its famous south elevation had more in common with a French palace than a government building. What began life as the headquarters of the Admiralty had passed to the MoD and, since 1964, served various government functions.

For Mike, his return to the Old Admiralty Building was less daunting than his entry into the adjacent building. Returning through the passageway was possible, but he couldn't risk being observed. He left Admiralty House, his smart suit showing no signs of his recent exit through a window or crossing layers of hedging. He headed for the north entrance of the Old Admiralty Building, where he was stopped by a guard and checked for ID.

According to the ID card clipped to the left side of his suit, the man was Captain Michael Hansen, DOB 7 June 1987, an officer in the Parachute Regiment based primarily at St Athan. Though technically the data was out of date, Mike knew that nothing had been left to chance and that the details on the pass would withstand any close visual examination. After checking the ID photograph, the guard moved to one side and saluted, "Good morning, sir."

Inside, the sights were familiar. In contrast to the grand exterior of white colonnades and red brick that sparkled in the late-morning sunshine, the interior was surprisingly unassuming. Rather than the expected sprawling chambers and the trappings of the upper class and wealthy, tall corridors with substantial doors echoed with the constant buzz of conversation. Most of the rooms were offices, displaying only the occasional poster or piece of artwork to interrupt the blank expanse of plain walls. The dress code varied considerably. Where once, an admiral could have been seen talking to a plump man with a hard round face drinking a large brandy, the modern reality was suits, uniforms, dresses and casuals.

Though some things had changed, others had not. A small lift shaft located off one of the main corridors was easily missed by anyone in a hurry. Its appearance was dated, even by the standard of others in the building. Like the American films of old, instead of imposing double doors, the inside was guarded by mechanical grilles that chimed as they closed. On reaching the lift, Mike swiped his key card and pressed the only available button: LG.

Lower ground.

As the descent ended, the grille opened to a dimly lit corridor lined with oak-panelled doors. Unlike the passages above, there was no echo of background noise. The walls were lead-lined and reinforced so that even the constant sound of London's heavy traffic at ground level could not be heard.

Mike remembered the first time he had visited the corridor. Despite having Kit for company, the feeling had been one of intense apprehension, a strange mix of claustrophobia and intimidation. According to the official PR information, the rooms had been built as Anderson shelters in 1939, though their appearances had changed since. Like the Admiralty citadel off Horse Guards Road and the spaces beneath the Treasury where

Churchill had mapped out operations, this maze of corridors and rooms was strictly private.

Knowledge of their existence was limited to a select few.

Stopping outside a strong oak door, the like of which implied entrance to a redundant cellar, Mike knocked, a distinct low pattern. Moments later, a heavy key turned in a lock, and an eye slit opened to reveal brown, intently focused eyes that carried an unmistakable air of authority. The door opened, and the first impression was confirmed. The man standing before him was in his late sixties and dressed impeccably in a suit. Like himself, he had started his career as a Red Beret before rapid progress through the civilian ranks of the MoD saw it end as the Department's Permanent Undersecretary of State.

His name was Ian Atkins.

Nodding at the commander, Mike entered a familiar room with an extensive array of electronic equipment. The silence of the corridor was replaced by the sound of voices of numerous different nationalities as their messages were intercepted and recorded by sophisticated communications monitoring receivers. Sixteen chairs surrounded a familiar circular table with an emblem identical to that in the room in Charlestown. In one of the chairs sat Kit, minus his glasses, sipping a cup of tea.

"I take it you found the place, okay?"

Mike grinned. The room always brought back memories of his first visit when he got lost leaving the toilet.

Atkins locked the door. Like the Director of the White Hart, he had the physique and bearing of a proud and senior military officer. After briefly scrutinising Mike's appearance through his rimless spectacles, he asked, "How did it go?"

"Entrance was easy. A mobile phone had recently been used, and the TV set to external, most likely a mobile phone or tablet hook up for a conference call. According to the call register on his phone, a conversation took place last night, ending at 23:00 hours. Phil is looking into tracing the recipient."

The Bordeaux Connection

The former head of the MoD nodded and raised his left eyebrow, causing the lines on his forehead to thicken. "Good. Even if it's nothing, at least it will verify what he's been doing with his time."

"There was nothing else on his mobile." Mike removed the flat black USB drive from his belt. "Then again, maybe Phil can find something I missed."

Atkins picked up the black object and turned to a stand-alone iMac on the far side of the room. As government computer systems were a magnet for hackers, the White Hart had always used Apple Macs built to their own specifications. And installed with the most highly effective anti-hacking software.

"Three calls yesterday, two lasting less than seven minutes." Atkins adjusted his glasses. "All different numbers. All mobile devices. One a number typically associated with France."

Mike watched the data come up on the screen in front of him. "Phil reckons he should be able to listen in from now on." He turned to Kit, whose expression was surprisingly breezy. "What about you?"

"Interesting, actually. All that history – you'd have loved it. Did you know Henry VIII used to get up at 5 a.m. to play tennis?"

"He also spent half his life trying to find a good divorce lawyer." He grinned. "Any problems with the office?"

"No, not really. I was able to log on to his computer easily enough and download the contents of his hard drive. I suppose it might take a while before IT knows the results."

Mike recognised IT was a reference to Phil. "Anything concrete?"

"Not particularly. His case contained nothing important. I put a wire beneath the flap, just in case, so if he does happen to let anything slip at the wrong time, then that would be unfortunate for him."

"How was his office?"

"Probably the same as his apartment. Smart but boring."

That just about sums it up. "Any nice upcoming holidays or dinner plans?"

"Opera tickets in the top drawer. It seems the Deputy PM has a particular love for Dvorák."

"When are they for?"

"Tonight, actually. Covent Garden. Maria said she'd try and get us fixed up."

"Great, just what I want." He turned to Atkins. "How about Jay and Marcus?"

"Nothing of importance. Wilcox searched Dorneywood top to bottom. Actually had the whole place to himself. Apart from a few ambiguous toys that we believe belonged to Mr Hughes's predecessor, there was nothing there. Found an old croquet set."

Mike laughed. "How about the apartment?"

"Iqbal completed a sweep of Knightsbridge in record time." He looked at Mike inquisitively through his lenses. "And a bloody good job too. You can just imagine the consequences if he'd been found snooping around a £1 million property in Knightsbridge."

"With his accent, I'm guessing he'd feel quite at home," Mike said.

"Assuming he had the chance to explain himself," Kit said.

"Any news on Randek?" Mike asked Atkins.

"Nothing definite, but he's unlikely to have made it to France yet. It can't be ruled out, of course, that he may have docked somewhere and taken a flight elsewhere. GCHQ believe they might have something from a hotel room – nothing positive. The PM has been fielding questions all morning. He will address the press again at noon. Most of the talk in the Commons has centred on Edinburgh. Unsurprisingly, the opposition had already been made aware of the two arrests. As far as I'm aware, there's been no mention of individual names."

"How about the culprits?" Mike asked.

"Well, nothing came up in the live debate. Of course, neither the PM nor the Foreign Secretary would be foolish enough to open a can of worms live on television, no matter how hard the leader of the opposition might try. As far as the public is concerned, the situation in Edinburgh has already been blown up out of all proportion, and we're dealing with nothing more than organised crime."

"Any comparisons to 7/7?"

"As a matter of fact, the Foreign Secretary compared it to the 2011 riots."

Mike nodded. A politician's answer. "How about the press?"

"The Cabinet Office has been peppered with questions, as has the MoD. The museums in Edinburgh are passing on all queries to Scotland Yard. The main fear north of the border seems to be mob violence. The authorities are refusing to label it a terrorist attack."

"Why should they?" Kit asked. "Even on the night itself, it was the local police who cleaned up the mess. As far as I'm aware, the military wasn't even called."

"Be that as it may, I think it's fair to say they were aware. They're probably in the same situation as us. There, but not seen. It's at times like this that security must remain watertight. Any hint of a leak . . ."

"But there hasn't been one yet?" Kit asked.

Atkins looked back with a firm expression. "I'd like to think most people in our organisation understand the business they work in, don't you?"

Mike sat down in the nearest seat, three along from Kit. He looked enviously at Kit's warm cup of tea and licked his dry lips. "Any orders from the PM?"

"No, the Director caught him for ten minutes on the line at 06:30; for obvious reasons, it hasn't been possible to speak to him since. Mr White wants surveillance on the Deputy PM and his wife to remain ongoing. The wife is currently relaxing in Knightsbridge. Iqbal himself saw her return within moments of his leaving the building. He's still in the vicinity. As far as we're aware, she's not left since."

"You think she'll be joining her husband at the opera?" Mike asked.

"Probably," Kit said. "Though the tickets weren't named."

"The tickets had most likely been a gift. I understand from the number the box is on permanent reserve, almost like a grace and favour," Atkins said.

"I take it if we go, we'll get no such favours?"

"Unless the PM has a trick up his sleeve," Mike said.

"Otherwise, it's the stalls." Kit grinned.

Mike guessed as much.

Atkins took a seat opposite them. "As I'm sure you'll both appreciate, if you do manage to gain entry, your purpose will be solely to observe. Any hint of trouble will only escalate matters. Even opera critics aren't illiterate."

"What if we get lucky?" Mike asked.

"Now steady on, Michael. After all, we are here to work."

Ignoring Kit, Mike asked, "Suppose Mrs Hughes is present, and we so happen to have a moment alone. Then what? We do nothing?"

"Well, that's hardly likely in an opera house. Even if you were alone, you'd probably have some fat Czech woman bellowing in your ear. As a matter of fact, I'd say keeping your distance is the priority. Any suspicion that she's under surveillance and the PM would have a minor crisis on his hands. Not to mention a divided Cabinet."

Mike accepted the point. "Very well. So does that mean we have the afternoon off?"

"In the meantime, you'll be staying here, if that's what you mean?" Atkins pointed to the far wall, a cramped space with bunk beds that had been put in for their predecessors at the height of the wartime Cabinet. "You'll find a spare pair of uniforms in the wardrobe, as well as a range of tuxedos and dinner jackets. After the week you've had, I suggest you both use the opportunity to catch up on some sleep."

Paris
17:00 Central European Standard Time

The narrow back streets of Paris had never been intended as tourist spots. Even for the most adventurous, they were the last places a stranger would head for, even in the middle of the day.

Walking the streets as dusk began to fall, Fabien Randek showed no signs of a man with something to worry about. After the life he'd had so far, one compromised robbery would hardly make much of a difference. As fate had had it, he'd managed to avoid detection as his two countrymen were being picked up. Like most times in his life, luck had shone upon him when it mattered. He hadn't been in the harbour at the decisive moment. He'd been on the phone.

Talking to a man about opera.

As the sun began to set on the other side of the Eiffel Tower, the cobbled streets took on a different feel. The stones were darker than usual; a quick shower that had passed as soon as it came had coated the hard surface with slippery moisture. Dusk had a timeless quality in the city; locals used to say it was at twilight when the past and the present came together.

Even in this less wealthy neighbourhood, the buildings were a hallmark of the city's post-revolution past. Rumour had it the series of former trade shops, whose purpose had spanned every guild, still sat on the ruins of historical sights. If the stories were to be believed, the street had known everything from wineries to blacksmiths. On the site of what was now a butcher's shop, a prison had stood in former times.

As Randek made the familiar walk along one particular street, ignoring the range of vehicles parked on both sides, he became aware of a pervading quietness that he was not used to. Few people were out, either on the roads or on the pavement. He knew the reason. Frenchman, Englishman, Scot, Czech, it made no difference. Everyone was watching, be it first hand or on a TV in their kitchen or living room.

The eyes of the world were firmly on the UK.

Next door to the old butcher's was another building of similar style but a different purpose. Experience told him the interior would be in character with the outside: a quaint bookshop run by one of the most established families in the area. The sign above the door had been there for years, the name recognisable to everyone in the neighbourhood. The former owner had been respected, particularly among the most learned.

A trait inherited by his son.

A substantial door occupied a space between red brick walls, darkened by past pollution. On one side of the entrance was a doorbell, and within the door itself, a small glass panel displaying a sign reading *Fermé*: closed. As he looked closer, he saw a second, smaller note.

Use the rear entrance.

Following the instructions, Randek took the detour to the end of the street and along a narrow alleyway behind the row of buildings. For the first time, evidence of squalor revealed itself: rubbish jutting up above garden fences, the smell reminiscent of a landfill. On reaching the bookshop, he found a small open gate leading to a path. Unlike its neighbours, the surface, though severely weathered, appeared in better surroundings. A bizarre selection of keepsakes from the city's past decorated the way, along with a profusion of brightly coloured pot plants. Many of the possessions of the present owner's father had been turned into ornaments. Items from watering cans to looms stood like miniature statues, a quaint feature that he attributed to the esoteric personality of the owner.

From the rear, the shop itself was far from impressive. The brickwork was dated and looking, in parts, in some danger of collapse. A second door, blue and glass framed, was similar in appearance to the one at the front and alongside double doors that led down into the ground. Neither was open, but he knew one would be unlocked. It was the entrance the owner preferred, out of sight, out of mind.

He knocked, waited, and knocked again. The second time he heard a voice.

He entered.

It was the one place in the city where he had always felt comfortable. His grandfather once told him that those who chose to walk abroad among their fellow man would always gain a place in the hearts of the people. In thirty years, he'd never disputed it. Experience told him it was the only part of Paris, the only part of the world, where a man of his background and family could walk in complete safety. The only place in Paris where he could use his real name. In other circles, he went by Christophe Blanc as it provoked little ill feeling. His typically French dark hair matched the photograph on Blanc's driving licence but differed substantially from the shaven-headed, stubbled individual who appeared on Randek's. Their ages in both were indeterminate, most likely over thirty, yet whether by two years or twelve was anyone's guess. Blanc's height was on file as half an inch more and his shoe size one larger; he achieved both with the aid of an insole. The rest was down to him and to fate. Thanks to his diet, he was now slightly heavier, the extra mass mostly around his thighs and biceps. The last thing he wanted was to gain mass anywhere else.

In his occupation, fitness was essential.

Randek, or Blanc, descended the wooden steps, his footfalls causing a prolonged creak as his size twelve footwear pressed down on the rotting wood. On reaching the bottom, he entered a familiar and stony cellar. The bricks were damp; they had been put in in an unsympathetic mix after the war, with the foundations of the building lost in the Revolution. The cellar gave off a distinct smell, not squalor, but even after all these years, he couldn't quite put his finger on the source. In the corner of the room, several bottles of red wine, mainly from the Poitou-Charentes region, were stacked in rows of three. Alongside were several containers that had once been used for bread or cheese. It was as if the smells of all these things had come together over the years in a way that could never happen again.

Something that belonged only there and in the depths of hell.

There were no windows in the cellar; the only light was artificial; a single forty-watt bulb dangled from the centre of the ceiling. The dim light of the solitary bulb illuminated furniture that had once belonged in the living room above. A rigid antique wooden chair was currently in use. Its occupant, it appeared from his physical features, was probably old enough to remember its creation. His grey hair had entirely receded on top, and what remained matched the colour of his eyes. His beard was full but no longer thick; its appearance had become dishevelled. His thin physique exaggerated the features of his bones, most of which were crippled by arthritis. He looked at Randek through small glasses perched, as always, on the end of his nose.

Randek stopped several metres away with folded arms. "Why must we always meet down here?" he asked. "Even the British Security Service would not be stupid enough to neglect to search an antiquarian's cellar."

He walked closer, detecting that the old man wasn't in any mood to reply.

"Jeremy and Serge are taken. I saw them led away with my own eyes. Fortunately, their property was not all seized."

He removed a manuscript from his black rucksack and waved it in the man's face. The bookseller waited, his grey eyes a milky white in the dim light.

"Do you have the map?" the man asked.

"I have the book."

"Where is it?"

Randek removed a second item from the rucksack he'd been carrying for the past two days and passed over the dense, hardback shell. The old man took both books and examined them one at a time. The title of the first confirmed a Scottish pedigree dating back to the old clan system.

The second, for now, was of greater interest.

Putting the first to one side, he took the second book and felt the spine with thin leathery hands. He blew the dust and cleaned it with a delicate brush before turning to the first page.

The text was handwritten, which was a good sign; if the rumours were true, the secrets only existed in the original. It was written in English, the handwriting elongated.

Also a good sign.

Randek watched with folded arms. "Well? You understand?"

The old man adjusted his glasses and reluctantly looked away from the book. "In matters such as these, there are no rules. Even the plausible must be taken as possible conjecture in the absence of firm proof." He turned to the later pages. While the early ones had been laid out consistently, four-line stanzas, iambic pentameter, and occasionally illustrated by quill-penned drawings, the last pages were blank.

"Well?" Randek pushed.

"If the reports are correct, we're talking not of a simple layout but a geometric puzzle. Written in a language known only by one who would understand."

Randek was unimpressed. "The boss has very high hopes. Lifelong dreams. Are you, Sébastien, going to be the one to disappoint him?"

The old man was unfazed. "Your boss is not the man you think he is. He understands only too well. There are no rules, nor can I make any promises. The author was a genius. One in a position to know what others did not."

He rose to his feet and walked to the far corner of the room where a second antique desk had been placed, its frame showing the effects of past woodworm. There was a further light source on the surface in addition to two unlit candles, both of which he lit after striking a match.

Randek approached, watching over the man's shoulder. The book was now lying on the desk, open towards the end.

"What are you doing? The wax will get everywhere."

"Shhh." The bookseller opened the second of his drawers, removed a swab from an unopened tin and placed the tip to the flame. Satisfied it was warm, he lowered his hand to the final page and brushed delicately across the blank page. Below his hand, he felt the temperature of the paper rise as it became exposed to heat. Finished, he did the same to the opposite page.

"What are you doing?" Randek asked, prepared to remove his semi-automatic pistol and shoot the old man there and then. The theft had taken months: the planning, the negotiation, the execution . . . the risk . . .

As he looked down at the tome, he noticed things had changed. The final pages, seconds earlier appearing murky yellow, tarnished by the brown stains of what he guessed were once burn marks, now revealed something more visible. Initially, the outlines were faint before becoming stronger. Then, finally, fully comprehendible.

Randek was lost for words; it was as if a great secret had been revealed to him, a doorway opening before him. He turned to the old man, who looked back. A smug smile formed across his thin features.

"Would you like to make the call, or shall I?"

Covent Garden, London
18:58

The car dropped them off on Russell Street, just off Wellington Street, close to the Strand. Taking advantage of a rare free parking bay on the side of the road, the dark-haired driver pulled up alongside a white hatchback and reverse-parallel parked into the space.

The car was a Bentley, one of the finest in the fleet. The order's selection was wide ranging: three-door hatchbacks to six-figure supercars. It was a profession where reliability was essential. Most of the models were disposed of after three years. The MoD had ongoing contracts with most of the suppliers, which ensured trade-ins were always of value. Those they kept might have lost their monetary worth, but some provided different value. An eight-year-old hatchback might lack the glamour of a supercar, but there were certain places one didn't travel in a Ferrari or a luxury BMW. A Nissan Micra could be readily used in the confines of inner-city Liverpool and Glasgow without fear of attracting unwanted attention. In contrast, in Kensington or Monaco, the opposite might be true. If one of the more luxurious vehicles went missing every so often, they would frequently turn up in possession of the targets themselves.

Even the thefts could be of value.

The driver of the Bentley was named Jamal Iqbal, a Birmingham-born operative of Iranian descent with an accent that Kit joked was a cross between the Black Country and the Queen's English. Known by those in the order as Jay, he glanced at the passengers in the rear-view mirror. He used the opportunity to play with his gelled hair.

"You can do that all you want; you'll never be as attractive as I am."

Kit was sitting behind the driver, alongside Mike and dressed impeccably. A smart tuxedo clung tightly to his firm physique; his dark hair had been carefully blow-dried and gelled. Once again, he was wearing dark-framed spectacles, which did more than just improve his eyesight.

Jay grinned. "Saw a very dapper-looking geezer coming out the doors of that flat in Knightsbridge. Can't be sure, but I think I'd seen him with that Hughes bird in all the tabloids. Right good-looking, he was."

Mike smiled. "Was he as attractive as Kit, though, Jay?"

Jay looked again in the mirror. "Nearly, Mikey. Nearly."

Mike's appearance was almost identical to Kit's; from the shoes to the hair to the jacket, they could almost have been mistaken for twins. He glanced at his watch and compared it to the clock on the dashboard. 18:55.

"What time did you say this thing starts again?"

"Seven thirty, according to Maria," Jay replied, in truth uncertain. Not for the first time in recent weeks, Maria had come up with the goods. The tickets, as expected, were bottom of the range; Mike guessed they were probably for somewhere on the floor.

Through the rear left window, Mike made out the figure of an elegant woman with jet-black hair. She carefully looked both ways before crossing the street and entering the front passenger seat. She flicked her hair to her right and left and closed the door behind her.

"Good evening, gentlemen."

"Well, it is now." Kit was suddenly alert.

Ignoring him, Maria reached into her handbag and removed a large white envelope. "Here are your tickets." She passed them to Mike, who looked at them closely.

Dvořák – *Rusalka*, 7:30 p.m., stalls, Row T, Seats 5–6. There was no seating plan on the tickets.

Kit, meanwhile, quietly eyed Maria's smart appearance: a black cocktail dress, her long fingernails complementing the colour.

The Bordeaux Connection

"If I didn't know any better, I'd say you were trying to impress someone," Kit said.

Mike looked up from examining the tickets. "I assume at least someone will be coming with us?"

She smirked. "You really think the civil service is going to fork out for me to see the opera? You guys get all the luck."

"You can always come instead of Mike. I'm sure he wouldn't mind."

"We understand the Deputy PM is already inside and enjoying dinner with his wife," she replied. "Your seats are quite a distance from his, so I'm relying on you to find a way of keeping him in check."

"Shame the B2s couldn't shell out on getting us a box opposite. That way, we'd have had the best of both worlds, and you'd have been able to enjoy the opera with us."

"Unfortunately, it probably wouldn't have made a difference. This thing's been sold out for months."

"Rather good, is it?" Kit asked.

"Apparently so. Rumour has it even the director of the new Russell Crowe film failed to get a ticket."

Mike raised an eyebrow. "How did you manage?"

"Tried my luck with a few contacts. Failing that, I tried corporate. Finally, I tried the ticket office."

Kit laughed. "So we're sitting in someone else's castoffs?"

"Not exactly." She touched in her lipstick, using the sun visor mirror for assistance. "It actually turns out they have something called day tickets: about sixty that go on sale the day of the performance. In any case, I doubt you'll be sitting all the time. It's a big venue. Too big to survey everything in the boxes from the stalls."

"So why are we here?"

"We've got you both inside. We can't do everything. The rest is up to you."

"Keeping an eye on someone of his profile from the other side of an auditorium that holds 2,000 people is hardly my idea of anything."

"You prefer to be outside?"

"I'd prefer you were in."

She bit her lip and smiled. "I suppose I shouldn't be too cross with you. That little toy you installed in his briefcase – worked like a charm. We've been able to eavesdrop on everything. Including one little chat with the PM."

"I'm sure the PM won't approve of that."

"Well, he did tell Mr White to leave no stone unturned. If he gets upset, I'll leave you to do the explaining." She caught Mike's eye in the rear-view mirror. "That was some great work in the apartment, by the way. We've managed to trace one of the calls to a number in Bordeaux. Interestingly, Mr Hughes was at Dorneywood at the time, so we're still unclear who used the TV."

"Who else has access to his apartment?" Mike asked.

"Your guess is probably as good as mine at this point – better even. The most important thing is that we do know that Mrs Hughes and her husband are here tonight. Phil's phone tap came in useful after all."

"Anyone coming with them?" Mike asked.

"Nothing based on his conversation with the PM. However, the boxes on that tier hold four people. In my experience, they're rarely left unfilled."

"Someone in Number 70, I bet. I heard Dvořák playing while I was in the office."

That amused Jay. "I never had you down as being into classical. Classic fool, maybe."

Kit stared into Jay's eyes via the mirror. "Jay, there's a bus due in ten minutes; why don't you get under it?"

Maria laughed for the first time. "Could be a coincidence; I couldn't hear it clearly over the phone. Nevertheless, you might have a point. Our earlier suspicions that the box is on permanent reserve have been confirmed. If Mr Hughes does have an extra couple of guests, most likely they're either people close to him or fellow members of the Cabinet."

"No leads?" Mike asked.

"Even if there were, your job is solely to observe. There'll be an interval around 20:40. If Mrs Hughes does decide to leave her seat, make damn sure you keep a sharp eye on whoever she talks to. It's a long shot, but if she is involved, we must have our angles covered."

She checked her watch. 19:03.

"You two best be going. Enjoy the show. I'll be asking questions later."

Mike and Kit left the car and headed left where Russell Street ended, and Wellington Street and Bow Street joined. Maria had disappeared; the last Mike saw of her, she was heading south-east towards the Strand.

He assumed someone was picking her up.

The Royal Opera House was located in the Covent Garden area of London. Dubbed simply 'Covent Garden' by the locals, the 2,200-seater auditorium was on the south side of Bow Street in the north of the City of Westminster.

Mike had never visited the venue before. Like many of Westminster's world-renowned attractions, the façade was in the Georgian Palladian style with six grand columns supporting a triangular gable. The original house, as Mike understood from Kit and Google, had burned down, as had the replacement. The present-day construction was on the same site as the 1730s original and was internationally celebrated as the home of The Royal Opera, The Royal Ballet, the Royal Opera Chorus, and the Royal Opera House Orchestra.

Kit and Mike crossed the road to the north side of Bow Street, pausing briefly to look around. Night was falling. The uniform soft yellow glow of the streetlights was almost entirely obscured by the bright star-like quality of the illumination of the opera house.

John Paul Davis

The crowds had gathered. Suited gentlemen, bow ties set tightly around their collars, walked the street with pomp and ceremony. Many escorted well-dressed ladies towards the main entrance, some stopping to examine the famed Enzo Plazzotta statue of the Young Dancer before crossing the road. In the heavy volume of traffic, both vehicles and people, many drivers took advantage of the delays to allow their finely dressed occupants to alight right in front of the venue.

Mike felt out of place. Though visually he looked the part, the jacket, the shoes, the trousers, the shirt – according to Kit, the whole package was a £650 bill to the taxpayer – something about opera had never sat right with him. There was a buzz in the air, but different to what he was used to. There was no singing or chanting or men consuming lagers or hotdogs as he expected of a day at Villa Park or a frequent away day at another football ground. Nor was it his usual style of concert. Absent were the merchandise retailers, traders selling knockoffs out of a case while others queued for the real thing at five times the price; also missing were the touts offering to sell or buy.

It wasn't like the atmosphere he'd experienced the night before, either. Edinburgh had been unique, even compared to the other missions he'd been on. All the thieves had been armed. The cargo they had managed to salvage had been lined with stolen art and guns. He liked those missions above the others. They were the ones where you knew the score in advance. The ones where the enemy stood out: the targets, usually, self-explanatory.

Tonight, on the other hand, was the type he hated. Nothing compromised a mission like crowds; worse still, the highbrow. Somehow, they always managed to get in the way, a magnet for delays. As he crossed the road, a vastly overweight woman in a dark green dress made him stop in his tracks as she leaned in towards a stranger's baby as its mother wheeled the pram.

"Oh, isn't he the cutest?"

Bumping into her was unavoidable.

The Bordeaux Connection

"Excuse me." Mike nodded and looked away quickly, doing his best not to be diverted. Beside him, Kit saw everything.

"Subtlety, Michael. One should always buy a lady dinner first."

Inside, the opera house was filling up. The house lights were on, shining down from the gods, illuminating the aisles where people came and went in a steady flow. The stalls area was a sea of red, occasionally interrupted by groups of people chatting quietly and soaking up the atmosphere in the comfortable seats.

The stage was rich in colour: the elegant curtains were firmly shut, their maroon coatings complemented by gold linings. From the outer trimmings to the opulent furnishings, the character was ornately regal. The insignia of the Royal Family decorated both curtains in the bottom corner, and the house's coat of arms was sighted prominently above the stage and on the Royal Box on the grand tier.

Four boxes on, four padded chairs were presently unoccupied. There were no smartly dressed spectators sitting, chatting or browsing through a programme. Most of the guests on that floor frequented the stunning dining room, accessible only to those with relevant tickets. It was an old tradition in these parts.

The best way to enjoy opera was on a full stomach.

In a less crowded area in the old, vaulted dressing rooms, two men and their glamorous wives enjoyed a particularly intimate dinner. Unlike the popular restaurant on the amphitheatre deck and the famous Crush Room, decorated in the Flemish style of the 1600s, the small, white-walled room was reserved only for the select few. While the men were dressed as expected for the occasion, their smart suits of earlier that day replaced by elaborate tuxedos, the women had opted for cocktail dresses of different styles. The more flamboyant of the two, famed in certain circles for her non-thriftiness, wore a striking blue dress that complemented silver earrings that dangled beneath her brown hair. The appearance of the blonde woman, who sat alongside her husband and opposite the well-dressed man with balding grey hair, was far more modest. The subtle purple dress blended in well with the surroundings. Like most women present, she wore jewellery, but in lesser quantities. For Lavinia Hughes, it was a time for discretion. Even if the Deputy PM was aware of the carping and sniggering comments about her past life – particularly from members of the opposition – he knew his wife had heard them all before.

Perhaps invented some of them.

The Deputy PM glanced at his wife, her pink lipstick an unbroken seal, as she cleaned her palate with a sorbet. Tonight she looked at her loveliest. He smiled at her and glanced at the clock.

"The performance will be starting in twenty minutes."

The other man smiled. "Excellent. That leaves just enough time for dessert."

Backstage the hubbub was reaching fever pitch. Stagehands moved in every direction, costume girls ducked in and out of doors, making sure everything was perfect for the opening.

Most of the performers were still in their dressing rooms, their eyes focused on the mirrors or conducting voice exercises to make sure everything was perfect for the real thing. Most of the instruments were already set up in the orchestra pit, awaiting the arrival of the musicians.

The cellist had seen it all before, even in this venue. In a twenty-year career, he'd toured the world, experiencing everything from being an understudy to a stand-in conductor.

But not tonight. Instead, the padded seat that cushioned his back and lower body was reserved purely for customers. The left side of the stalls circle was a decent place to sit, all things considered. It was close to the orchestra and the stage and close to an aisle, but not too high up. In his experience, the grand tier was the best place to enjoy a performance; tonight, however, that would be more than just superfluous but potentially counterproductive. A view from higher up might be something that many would envy, but there was one thing the grand tier didn't facilitate so readily.

Escape.

9

Covent Garden, London
19:12

Mike felt a light tap on his shoulder as he headed for the main doors.

"I almost forgot; these are for you." Maria was standing behind him, holding a leather case. She passed it to him. "They might come in useful."

Mike opened it, revealing a set of opera glasses.

Kit was unimpressed. "How far back are we?"

A wry smile. "Phil said they'd come in handy. Enjoy the show, boys."

Maria disappeared amongst the crowd, heading north. Mike, meanwhile, removed the miniature binoculars from the case and examined them as they walked. Despite clear evidence of modern additions, including computerised features around the eyepieces, the style was typically 19th-century lorgnette, mother of pearl, and clearly original. There were buttons close to the right eyepiece; Mike pushed the first and was immediately lost for words. Out of keeping with the Victorian appearance, each eyepiece incorporated a 25x zoom, infrared and night-vision capability and a digital distance gauge.

He showed them to Kit. "At least one of us will be able to see the stage."

"In that case, you can be the one who keeps to the seats."

The lobby and foyer areas were packed, as were the gangways. An announcement came through the speaker system, accompanied by fanfare, informing the operagoers that the performance was about to begin and that guests should start making their way to their seats. Mike led the way. He followed the crowds and the signs along a narrow, carpeted concourse and through a doorway that led into the orchestra stalls.

The seats were exactly what Kit had expected. Row T, Seats 5 and 6, on the floor and close to the back. Though the seats were comfortable and the view clear, Kit guessed they were among the worst in the house.

Mike checked his watch. 19:27. Three minutes until the performance was due to begin. Above them, the grand tier, the balcony boxes and the amphitheatre were packed to capacity, the final influx of guests taking their seats. In front of them in the orchestra stalls, the ocean of red that had greeted the early guests was now a multitude of colour: dinner dresses, cocktail dresses, hats, scarves, fedoras, interrupted by consistent smatterings of penguin suits.

The large attendance aside, the first thing that caught Mike's attention was how lavish everything was. Every tier was gilded, painted with murals and illuminated by candelabra-style wall lights that caused a consistent glow effect. The lighting complemented the lining of the famous domed ceiling that reminded him of the basilicas in Rome. Maria had referred to the venue as the place where the magic happened.

The statement felt peculiarly apt.

Mike removed the opera lenses from the leather case and experimented with its capabilities. With the leading house lights on, the infrared and night-vision settings were both redundant, but the distance gauge worked perfectly. From their seats to the stage, the display read 38m; 33m to the beginning of the orchestra pit. The furthest point from their seats was the ceiling that fluctuated between the high fifties and low sixties.

He concentrated on the grand tier, the first tier from the ground. From what he had gathered from Maria, the Deputy PM and his wife were sitting in a box on the right side, four from the so-called Royal Box.

Three of the seats in that area appeared to be taken.

The Deputy Prime Minister had been in his seat less than a minute before he felt a hand on his shoulder.

"You know, I can't tell you how delighted I am we were able to do this. Dvořák has always been a weakness of mine, and this is the great man's best. Tell me, are you familiar with his work?"

The Deputy PM smiled, his eyes taking in the familiar features of the man sitting behind him. The man's name was Richard Pickering, formerly Secretary of State for Justice.

More recently appointed Foreign Secretary.

"Mozart and Handel have always been my favourites. Though I must admit, I've always had a soft spot for the *Sinfonia Number Nine.*"

"Ah, a connoisseur, I see. Have you seen it before?"

"The piece or the venue?"

"Well, both, I suppose."

"The opera house and I are old friends. Aunty Pat used to bring me here when I was a child. I must admit, I didn't share the same passion back then as I do now."

"How about for Dvořák?"

"Once, I think. Though again, I must confess whatever I saw, I now remember little of it." He turned fully in his seat. "You'll know far more, I expect."

Pickering smiled, his white teeth practically glowing against the lighted backdrop. "Compared to the average man, maybe. Then again, I have been told some in my constituency would consider a bar crawl in Prague a good alternative to sightseeing. But I daresay, I'm out of my depth in the current company."

The Deputy PM laughed graciously as he felt a presence to his right, his wife. She seated herself awkwardly and reached into her bag for her opera glasses.

"I was just telling Richard about my trips here when I was young. I suppose you attended more than I."

"I'm not ignorant if that's what you mean." She smiled. "At least, so my boyfriend keeps telling me."

The Bordeaux Connection

The Deputy PM looked over his shoulder. "I hope Rachel isn't long. I'd hate for her to be caught with the lights out."

The Foreign Secretary smiled. "You know, I did warn her about the menu. Woman's a terror for mussels."

Mike had spent the previous minute staring at Box 63 through the opera glasses. The view on full zoom was impressive. Phil had done a good job creating something with so little camera shake.

"Do you see anything?" Kit asked from his left.

Mike handed over the glasses. "See for yourself."

Kit removed his black-rimmed spectacles and put the opera lenses to his eyes. Sure enough, the Deputy Prime Minister was sitting in the front row alongside his wife, who was dressed impeccably in an elegant purple dress. Beyond them was a balding, grey-haired man, aged around fifty, attired in a black tuxedo.

"Well, I'll be."

Mike laughed. "I know; I should have thought after the day he's had, spending an evening in the company of the DPM would be the last thing he'd have wanted."

"Oh, I don't know. A Dvořák opera, nice company, an eight-course meal beforehand. An excellent place to discuss a few things." Kit paused, glancing at Mike. "They share a country retreat, don't they?"

"Chevening, a mansion in Kent. The DPM also shares Dorneywood with the Chancellor." Mike recalled his last conversation with Mr White and then the later ones with Maria, Phil and Atkins.

"I believe we have a friend who visited Dorneywood recently."

"Apparently, Dorneywood is his favourite. Found it interesting, I suppose?"

"I understand he found it as much to his liking as another of my friends did one in Knightsbridge." Kit looked over his shoulder and lowered his voice. "I wonder what they're saying."

"Was wondering the same thing. Maria said it worked – the phone, that is."

"It did. Phil has apparently been listening." Kit looked again over his shoulder and lowered his voice further. "However, between you and me, I don't think now is the time or the place to ask him any questions."

They both heard Phil's voice in their earpieces. "Nothing important. Apparently, Mrs Pickering has been forced to make an unscheduled pit stop."

Mike grimaced; Kit laughed.

"You know, I was wondering who the final seat was for. It would be unlike a man of his stature to arrive stag at a place like this." Kit leaned closer to Mike, peering again through the lenses. "Hope the poor dear is okay. After all, I'd hate for her to miss the beginning."

The voice in their ears said, "The Deputy PM just said exactly the same thing."

"A man after my own heart."

"They have rather strict rules here, apparently," Mike said. "If you arrive late, you can't enter until the interval."

"You're quite sure?" Kit asked.

"No. But it's what I've heard."

He looked at Mike and raised his voice. "So tell me, Michael, what motivated you to come here tonight?"

Mike grinned. "Does a man need a reason for indulging in some culture after a tough day at work?"

"Absolutely not. So have you been to the opera before?"

"Twice. We took my mother on Mother's Day once. *Carmen*."

"How lovely."

"Other than that, just musicals."

"*Sound of Music*? *Mary Poppins*?"

"*Blood Brothers*."

"Well, shag the vicar," Kit said, quoting a line from the production that Mike instantly remembered. "I remember studying the tale of the Johnstone twins at Harrow."

The Bordeaux Connection

"And I at secondary school. So what about you, Kitford? I hear attending the theatre was almost compulsory at Harrow."

"Yes, along with fagging."

"The cause of it, I heard."

Kit looked at Mike, suddenly annoyed. He held his tongue and looked again at Box 63. The Deputy PM focused on the stage; alongside him, his wife did the same through elaborate opera glasses. The Foreign Secretary sat in the row behind with his arms folded, a broad smile on his face. Mrs Pickering was still absent.

A bad case of mussels, apparently.

Kit reached beneath the seat. He'd bought a programme on the way in, which Mike was still to see. "I don't suppose you're familiar with the story?"

"*The Little Mermaid* – more or less anyway."

"You've seen it before?"

"Not personally, but I know it's the only one of his operas regularly staged outside the Czech Republic."

Kit laughed. "However are you still single?"

"You never fancied taking Sharon – or Maria, for that matter?"

The leading lights went down, and a gasp went up from the crowd. As the 2,200-seater auditorium became enclosed in darkness, the guide lights from the nearby aisles formed a sole romantic white glow around the outer rim as the stage was engulfed in light.

Kit changed the setting on the lenses to night vision. The wavy green backlight cut perfectly through the darkness, revealing the shapes of the three guests in Box 63.

"One day, maybe. However, I suspect tonight is unlikely to allow me to enjoy the performance."

Mike took the glasses from Kit and reverted his gaze to the box. "No, I think you may have a point."

In one of the public toilets on the grand tier, the wife of Richard Pickering heard a roar from inside the venue. According to her watch, the time was seven thirty exactly.

As usual, the opera started on time.

The toilets were deserted; she could sense the solitude even with the door closed. In the quiet surroundings, the sound of her mobile phone bleeping with the arrival of an incoming text message seemed louder than usual, causing her heart to palpitate. Adjusting her dress as she sat on the closed lid, she read the message.

Starting now. Hope your stomach's okay.

Of all the ideas her husband had ever come up with, this was easily her least favourite. Of all the operas she had to attend and miss with a fake stomach complaint, it had to be *Rusalka*. Even before they married, she'd always been partial to opera. And Dvorák. Still, she wasn't going to let him off that easy, she'd decided. He'd promised to take her to see it in Prague to make it up to her. She replied simply:

I'll be out in five minutes.

The plan had been discussed in detail. Five minutes meant twenty, and out meant out of the building. That gave her twenty minutes to wait.

With nothing to do but pretend to have a bad stomach.

The Deputy PM felt another light tap on his shoulder. "Rachel is feeling better; she'll be with us in a few minutes."

Hughes smiled and immediately returned his attention to the stage. A second round of applause went up as the curtains opened.

Forgetting about his colleague's absent wife, he folded his arms and relaxed deeper into his chair.

On the opposite side of the auditorium on the ground floor, the cellist was enjoying a perfect view. Despite their antique appearance, his opera glasses were capable of much, even if they weren't the most powerful or sophisticated in the room.

As the minute hand of his watch struck six, the smaller hand pointing midway between seven and eight, the main lights extinguished suddenly. While most of the guests focused on the stage, he glanced up and to his right at Box 63. The four-seat box on the first tier, empty just five minutes earlier, was now three-quarters occupied. Even from a distance, he recognised the faces. Each was a celebrity in their own right. Though some more so than others.

Through the night-vision scope, he made out the figure of the Deputy PM; he could tell from the man's lazy posture he'd enjoyed his meal and was in no hurry to leave his seat any time soon. Sitting alongside him, his wife was altogether more rigid and focused, her opera glasses fixed on the stage.

Behind him, the Foreign Secretary checked his watch before glancing across the auditorium uncannily in his direction. He couldn't decide if the Foreign Secretary could make him out or whether it was simply a coincidence.

Seconds later, he saw the man look down at his lap and almost immediately, he felt his phone vibrate in his pocket. Casually, he removed it and scanned the text.

The message was from him, the words as expected. He replied 'Yes', looked across the theatre and nodded. Through his opera glasses, he saw the Foreign Secretary was again focused on his phone. Then he looked in his direction, nodded and folded his arms.

19:31.

Leaving just fourteen minutes.

The Royal Opera House
19:40

The opera had been in full swing for almost ten minutes. The music was loud, the stage colourful, the story proceeding at speed. What was happening, Mike had no idea. Without paying attention to the subtitles, he didn't understand a word of Czech.

During that time, Phil's voice had come through twice in his ear. Hughes and Pickering had bantered briefly about Mrs Pickering's digestive system, though they'd remained quiet since the singing started. Mike had hogged the eyepieces, his attention alternating between the stage and Box 63. There was still no sign of Mrs Pickering. Nor, as far as he could tell, was anybody moving their lips.

He guessed little would change until the interval.

Kit spoke in his ear, "Right, down to business. What can you see?"

Mike took a further look through the lenses. The Deputy PM and his wife remained engrossed in the production. In contrast, the Foreign Secretary was concentrating on his phone.

He passed Kit the glasses. "I think one of the guests must have something else on his mind."

Kit adjusted the settings. In addition to the night-vision and infrared settings, there was also one labelled X. Using it for the first time, he saw various objects highlighted in various colours. X clearly stood for X-ray. "Well, uneventful though it may be, at least we know the gimmicks work."

"I'm surprised that boy never got picked up by NASA."

"Still time, Michael. You know, during his thinner days, he spent some time at MIT."

"Really?"

The Bordeaux Connection

"Indeed. Then later, as an intern at Silicon Valley. You never know. He's the kind of chap people at Cape Canaveral go for."

"Not to mention the FSB."

Kit laughed. "Either way, it'd be a shame to lose him."

"Certainly would. You did say you've been here before?"

"Yes, my Sharon has always been rather partial to a bit of culture."

"How easy is it to get to the boxes?"

"Difficult. There's staff everywhere, particularly along the aisles and on the stairs. They don't like it when you move during a performance. Different during the interval."

Mike expected as much. He remembered what Maria had told him. Her job was only to get them in. The rest was up to them.

"You think we should stay here?"

"You have a better idea?" Kit looked around. "I suppose we could always climb up to the balcony."

Mike grinned. "You volunteering? Sadly, I've never been blessed with great grip."

"No, I think that sort of thing is best left to Bear Grylls. Our orders were to keep watch. For now, that shouldn't be too difficult."

The Foreign Secretary felt a further vibration in his pocket. Removing his phone, he read the latest message in his inbox and leaned close to the seat in front of him.

"I'm just going to check on Rachel."

The Deputy PM smiled and waved him away.

Mike saw movement at the back of the box.

"He's moving," he whispered to Kit.

"Who?"

"Pickering. His wife is still absent."

"How about the others?"

"Still engrossed by the magic." Through the night-vision setting, he saw the bearded Deputy Prime Minister barely acknowledge his fellow cabinet minister as the Foreign Secretary rose to his feet. What he saw next surprised him.

"Hello?"

Kit was intrigued. "What?"

"Seems our friend here was looking at someone across the floor." Mike scanned the stalls circle, the inclined area of seating to the left of the floor seating. A man was leaving a seat three rows back, two blocks from the orchestra pit. Mike zoomed in and saw the man attempting to pass four well-dressed people who separated him from the nearest exit.

"Where?" Kit whispered. "Show me."

"Here." Mike passed over the opera glasses. "Guy with the beard. Third row at the back."

Kit focused on the area Mike had described. Only one person was standing in that section; sure enough, the man was bearded and dressed in a smart tuxedo complemented by a bow tie. He'd made it to one seat from the end, apologising and smiling politely at the visitors as he passed.

"You're quite certain they were looking at each other?"

Knowing for sure was impossible. "I saw Pickering nodding in his direction." He retrieved the opera glasses and focused on the empty seat the Foreign Secretary had recently vacated. "You never know. Maybe they're preparing to meet."

"In that case, I think one of us better check it out. Better safe than sorry and all that. You stay here and listen in."

Mike nodded and put his finger to his ear while Kit casually left his seat and made his way swiftly to his left.

"My apologies," Mike overheard him say twice before leaving Row T and heading for an exit to the rear of the stalls. Gazing through the powerful lenses, he saw the man with the beard depart along an aisle between two blocks of tiered seating.

Mike guessed the exits all led to the same concourse area.

Kit turned right on leaving the auditorium and took a moment to familiarise himself with his surroundings. The concourse was in keeping with what he'd seen of the lobby. A stylish combination of red carpet complemented by dark brown wooden walls intercepted at regular intervals by cosy yellow wall lights.

The concourse was largely deserted. A well-dressed usher nodded and smiled at him as he passed, while a bald punter wearing a red bow tie and a smart tuxedo followed him through the exit and headed straight for the gents. He remembered from his research that the opera house adjoined the Paul Hamlyn Hall on this side. The stunning glass structure had been reinvented from a dilapidated floral hall to a champagne bar and restaurant.

The area was presently closed and deserted.

The man with the beard emerged to the right, walking confidently in his direction. Kit got out his phone as the stranger passed, avoiding eye contact.

He'd timed the move perfectly. A split second can be a long time, particularly if you're a trained operative. The man was about five feet eight in height possibly of French descent; he estimated fourteen and a half stone in weight. Kit detected a strong scent from the man's neck; he immediately recognised it as *Bleu de Chanel*, a personal favourite. Kit felt it was in keeping with the man's smart appearance but not with his character. Though nicely trimmed, the beard was capable of hiding the odd scar or mole. Indents into the bridge of his nose suggested recent wearing of spectacles or sunglasses.

As the man disappeared after making his way around the curvature of the concourse, Kit turned and followed him. He saw the man again as he approached the doors to the lobby, apparently admiring the architecture as he walked. Kit recognised the area from their earlier entry, the grand façade of the Bow Street entrance largely hidden by the ceiling of the 19th-century foyer. Rather than heading for it, the man strolled towards the Pit Lobby and passed the grand staircase.

The cellist had seen the Foreign Secretary's nod. Even without the aid of his powerful opera glasses, the gesture had been clearly visible. Within seconds, a new text message came through, the subtle vibration evident against his right thigh.

Even to the nearest second, everything was on schedule.

The Foreign Secretary appeared along the corridor in front of him, instantly recognisable.

"I trust Mrs Pickering will make a speedy recovery?" the cellist said as their stride patterns overlapped. "It would be a great tragedy should she miss this superb event."

"A gentleman must never get in the way of a woman and a good meal, Everard." He steered the cellist away from the lobby doors, checking they were not being observed. "I trust everything is set."

"I trust you left your jacket in the place we had previously agreed?"

The Foreign Secretary was clearly wearing his jacket. "I took the liberty of leaving the liquid beneath the seat. I think it's highly unlikely it will cause any suspicion."

"The boss has never been known for tolerating alterations to his plans."

"Well, on this occasion, your boss will have to make do. If any remains were to be found in the pocket, I stand to personally incriminate myself. Besides, one doesn't throw away things from Savile Row without good reason."

The cellist was unimpressed. "I can think of no worse reason than to compromise something so delicate over something so unnecessary."

The Foreign Secretary's face reddened. "Well, that's hardly your concern, is it? I mean, it's all right for the rest of you. You don't have the world and his wife lying in wait for your latest slip-up. Your every breath scrutinised."

"I trust the Prime Minister was satisfied by the events of the day?"

Pickering checked his watch, stern faced. "Eight minutes. Long enough for me to get comfortable on the john. I don't expect to see or hear from you ever again. Is that clear?"

"May I say it's been a pleasure doing business with you, sir."

The Bordeaux Connection

Kit kept his distance. His view was good enough to see that a conversation was underway, but he was too far away to be able to listen in. Staying on the left side of the concourse and with his back to one of the walls, he spoke into his mouthpiece, calling Mike by his White Hart codename.

"Grosmont, can you hear me?"

A mumbled reply confirmed he had.

"Seems congratulations are in order. You were right, after all. The Foreign Secretary and the creature from the black lagoon are having a conversation just off the Pit Lobby as we speak."

In row T, Mike whispered into his hand, "Any idea what about?"

"No. I'm too far away. How's his right honourable friend?"

Mike checked Box 63 through his opera glasses. "Pickering's wife's still absent; the others haven't moved."

Kit smiled at a smartly dressed woman as she passed him, heading for the toilets. He held his phone to his ear as a diversion.

"Keep an eye on them; I'm going to stay with our friend here. Let me know if the Foreign Secretary returns to his seat."

"Roger that."

Kit spoke again immediately. "You still listening, Phil?"

"Loud and clear."

Kit unlocked the keypad of his satellite phone by inserting an eight-digit code and casually pointed the camera lens in the direction of the Foreign Secretary. "I'm going to send you a few photographs. Let me know what you think."

At the other end of the line, Phil experienced over ten seconds of silence before hearing a bleeping sound, indicating a new email had arrived in his laptop's inbox. He opened it and saw there were photographs attached. He counted seven in total.

"Wow."

"I assume I don't need to clarify any of this?"

Phil rubbed his chin, a wry smile emerging across his face. The photos captured a conversation taking place between two well-dressed figures. The Foreign Secretary was quickly recognisable; even from one side, he had one of those faces that was almost impossible to mistake.

"I take it this is recent?"

"Yes, matter of fact, the button's still warm." Kit moved slightly nearer; the Foreign Secretary and his unknown accomplice remained partially visible. "They're still speaking; I can't hear what about."

"Shame you couldn't have dropped one of my bugs into his jacket this morning."

"Yes, well, unfortunately, I'm not clairvoyant, am I? How about the other man? I assume he's known to us?"

"I'll run his face through the database right now," he said, noticing that the third photograph, in particular, had caught him face-on. "You're certain he didn't see you?"

"I was very discreet."

Phil didn't doubt it. "Stay in touch. Hopefully, I'll have some good news for you very soon."

Kit put his phone away and waited patiently, using the curvature of the walls to stay hidden from sight. The meeting appeared to be breaking up. He saw the Foreign Secretary move confidently along the corridor, following it before heading right: the gents. The man with the beard loitered for several seconds before deciding against using the facilities.

Instead, he followed the concourse south.

Kit passed the doors to the lobby, keeping his distance. The concourse on the west side mirrored that of the east: carpeted, yellow lights glowing against wooden surroundings and decorated with various pieces of opera-related memorabilia.

The man with the beard strolled on. A glass exit led out close to the piazza, a designated smoking area. Kit watched him leave through the electronic door and light a cigarette.

The Bordeaux Connection

He heard Phil's voice in his ear. "Well, wonders never cease. We've got an exact match. Everard Payet, aka Patrice Everard, aka Matthieu Deminy, aka Hans Strum, aka Igor Viktal."

Kit concealed himself from view, using the nearby wall as cover. He removed his phone from his pocket, again using it to disguise his conversation. "That's one heck of a list of names."

"Trust me, this fella has one heck of a pedigree. Former French military, including two years in the Foreign Legion. He's also worked as a paralegal, a manager at a supermarket, a petrol station attendant, and a maître D' at a five-star restaurant. On top of all that, he has over twenty years' experience touring the world as an acclaimed cellist and violinist. No known criminal record in the last five years except for three points on his licence here two years ago and for smoking pot four years ago. Forty-two, wife deceased, alleged connections with Randek and another three criminal gangs. Home city is Bordeaux."

"Anything concrete with Randek?"

"Matter of fact, he has a child with his sister."

"You're joking?"

"Apparently not. Not that I've had a chance to check this out in detail. According to this, he's a code amber on the watch list. Thanks to your photos, I'm guessing he might even be in line for a promotion."

"What about last known whereabouts?"

Phil entered a search into the main terminal. "Wow. According to passport control, a certain Matthieu Deminy was booked on a flight to Edinburgh from Stockholm the morning of the explosions."

Kit was shocked. "Was he on it?"

"Unclear. If he was, the possibility can't be ruled out he was the second guy on the boat with Randek. I'll let you know if anything shows up . . . where are you now?"

"West concourse."

"What's happening?"

John Paul Davis

"Nothing really. Everard III has gone for a ciggy just off the piazza. His right honourable friend, the lavatory."

Phil grinned. "You might want to get back to your seat. You're missing the best part."

The sarcasm was evident. "I'll get Grosmont to tell me about it." He glanced quickly through the glass door, seeing the man with the beard was still there. "Why would the Foreign Secretary be speaking with him? Here, in public. Perhaps we're looking at this the wrong way."

"What way did you have in mind?"

"Well, it's perfectly obvious. The PM has instructed us to keep tabs on a certain member of his Cabinet. Maybe he's asked us to watch the wrong member."

"You saw the photo of Hughes's wife. She was the one with Randek. She was guilty of the theft."

"Was the Foreign Secretary there?"

"In Somerset? As a matter of fact, there's a photo of the four of them standing in the garden."

"Remind me. Those two do share a residence together?"

"Indeed they do. It's called Chevening House. A country estate in Kent. Apparently, they're good friends."

"Perhaps too good. They ever stay there at the same time?"

"Probably. It's a big place. One hundred and fifteen rooms; grounds spread over 3,500 acres."

Kit didn't bat an eyelid. "More than enough for two big egos to share, yet without arousing suspicion of why they should be there together . . . has it been swept?"

"Not yet."

"I suggest that be made a priority. Make sure the King is aware of this before the night is out."

Richard Pickering cautiously entered the toilet on the west side, grateful to find himself alone. He remembered from his previous visit there was a long line of cubicles on one wall opposite an even greater selection of urinals that smelt of lemon air freshener.

The Bordeaux Connection

He chose the cubicle one from the end and sat down on the closed seat. He'd felt his phone vibrate in his pocket during his conversation with the cellist. He checked it and saw that it was from his wife. The simplest of questions.

Where are you?

He replied with the simplest of answers.

Concourse. Same place as you.

The Foreign Secretary took a deep breath and returned his phone to his pocket. The time on the display confirmed it was 19:49, meaning he'd missed just four minutes of the performance. And six minutes until time was up.

Six minutes till everything changed.

In his long career, Richard Pickering had become used to dealing with stress. Ten years as a civil servant and later a counsellor had been the perfect apprenticeship to a career in Westminster. Eight years on the backbenches had been rewarded by four as a minister: Secretary of State for Transport, Secretary of State for Justice, and then the most recent, his greatest rise.

Foreign Secretary.

As a young man, he had aspired to do what was good and great; as a middle-aged man, he had learned the grim realities of what life in politics really involved. Like the cubicle around him, what started as a doorway to freedom now felt more like four walls closing in on him. Much had changed during the last year, most of it regrettable. That first trip to Europe. That first week in France.

His last as an honest man.

He felt another vibration in his pocket and rechecked his phone. One new message – again, his wife. He replied rapidly, the words barely registering. Three minutes. Soon it would be two.

The media would be talking about this for years.

The Royal Opera House
19:49

Any lingering interest Mike still had in the opera had well and truly evaporated. Even with the English subtitles, it failed to command his attention though quietly, he approved of the music. The famous scores and arias, the like of which he was surprised to recognise in part, had so far provided a palatable backdrop to what was fast becoming a tedious mission on the back of little sleep.

The Deputy PM remained seated in the same position, his eyes focused on the stage. To his right, his wife's body language was almost identical, her pretty face partially shielded by her opera glasses.

The row behind them remained vacant. While Mrs Pickering was still to appear at all, the Foreign Secretary had been missing for almost five minutes.

Still checking on his absent wife, Mike assumed.

Shielding his mouth, he spoke to Kit. "What's happening?"

The reply was crisp. "Turns out our friend with the beard is a most wanted man. I assume you heard what Phil had to say."

"I hear a lot of things. Where is he now?"

"Outside one of the doorways. Smoking something. Whatever it is, it looks legal. I certainly can't smell anything from the streets."

"How about Pickering?"

"Entered the facilities three minutes ago. Still to emerge."

Mike grinned. "Let's hope it wasn't the mussels."

"Any sign of his wife?"

"Negative. Haven't seen her all night."

"Not her night."

"You need any help?"

"No. You keep your eyes peeled on Hughes. Keep the frequency open. I might call you."

The Bordeaux Connection

"Roger that."

Mike lowered his hand and looked to his right and left. To his left, a woman in her mid-sixties was staring at him, seated one on from where Kit had been. He smiled at her politely and returned his gaze to the stage. He raised the opera glasses to his eyes and pretended to concentrate until the woman stopped looking.

About six seconds.

The eyepieces were incredible. While Mike had expected a Phil-built reconnaissance device that delivered beyond the military standard, the fourth setting he found particularly impressive.

Selecting the X, he zoomed in again on Box 63. The outlines of the Deputy PM and his wife appeared as unspecified balls of mass, surrounded by various shapes and colours. The physical properties of Box 63 were also exposed, the screen offering insights into the walls behind them.

For the first time, Mike made a mental plan of the entire floor. Some of the boxes had a set of steps leading down into them from the nearby corridor that matched what he had seen in the foyer. Wooden doors guarded them, casting the matching upholstery in shade. The walls of the corridor behind, whatever colour they were, were decorated with the usual artwork and memorabilia. The majority had been placed at equal intervals and around head height, complementing other pieces of furniture that he guessed were probably antique.

The corridor was deserted, which he'd expected; the Foreign Secretary and his wife aside, he saw no empty seats on that tier. If Kit was correct, the Foreign Secretary had chosen a toilet on the floor below.

Strange, considering signs for a public convenience were listed within metres of Box 63.

The seats behind the Deputy PM and his wife were not permanently fixed to the floor. The chair that had been occupied by the Foreign Secretary was slanted at a slight angle from where Pickering had made his recent exit.

Mike adjusted the zoom and focused on the chair. A strange light was flickering: small and yellow, seemingly coming from beneath the seat.

He covered his mouth, "Phil, I've got a question about the X-ray."

"Pretty impressive, don't you think? Bet you wish you'd have had one of these last night."

Last night probably wouldn't have made much of a difference, he mused. "I've got something coming up yellow."

"Where?"

"Box 63. Seems to be coming from underneath Pickering's seat."

"Yellow is your standard explosive feature. If you care to look down at your legs, your stuff should be the same colour."

Mike followed Phil's instructions and gazed down at his legs. A clear shade of yellow was visible from his left pocket, where he kept smoke dispensers, while a gun-shaped green was visible beneath his right trouser.

Neither perfectly matched what he saw in Box 63.

He spread out his search boundaries, taking in every box on the first tier before doing the same for the balcony boxes on the second, the amphitheatre on the third and finally, the stalls. Purple and grey appeared regularly; the shapes suggested mobile phones and wallets. He turned to his right, where an overweight gentleman wearing a tuxedo and glasses was too enthralled in the production to notice him. To his left, he clearly made out the contents of a handbag.

The woman was staring at him again.

He turned his head to his right. "What are the options?" he asked, keeping his voice low. "I'm seeing a lot of purple for phones and tablets. Is yellow definitely explosives?"

"We could be talking something that's merely highly flammable: a gas pipe, a fuel tank, maybe some highly unpleasant alcohol. What shape is it?"

The Bordeaux Connection

He adjusted the zoom and squinted. "Not sure. Based on this, it could be bottle shaped. You sure we aren't just looking at fizzy pop?"

"Unlikely. Unless someone has mixed some liquid explosives in with it. Where exactly is it?"

Mike maximised the zoom on the lenses. Despite being on the maximum zoom, the lack of shake was impressive.

"Beneath the chair behind the Deputy PM. Previously occupied by his good friend."

"Was it there before they arrived?"

"Couldn't tell you. I've only just discovered it . . . are we in danger?"

"It's tough to tell without seeing it up close. Ideally, I'd need to see a photo."

"Roger that."

Mike cleared his throat and lowered the opera glasses away from his eyes. To his left, the woman had finally resorted to concentrating on the opera.

He slowly got to his feet and headed left in the same direction as Kit.

"Excuse me," he said, forcing the spectators to get to their feet. As he reached the exit, he returned his attention to Box 63.

The yellow light was no longer visible at the new angle.

He accelerated through the exit. "Edward, we may have a problem. Something's showing up on the X-ray. Phil says it might be explosive."

Kit was still standing in the concourse, pretending to be on the phone. Everard was still outside, leaning against the glass, smoking his cigarette.

"I can hear every word, remember? And what the hell do you mean – might be explosive?"

"I'm getting something bright and yellow under the seat the Foreign Secretary had been sitting on. Whatever it is, Phil confirmed it probably isn't good."

Kit bit his lip, avoiding swearing. "All right, listen to me. Do whatever it takes to get to the grand tier. Survey it from as far away as you can. If you're as good as you think you are, he might not even notice you."

"Here's hoping. Phil, I'm going in. Unless I receive orders to the contrary."

"Grosmont. This is the King."

Mr White. "Sir . . ."

"You listen to me, Grosmont. Phil included these things for a reason. You saw what happened in Edinburgh. If there's even the slightest chance this thing is lethal, then several lives will depend on a successful diagnosis."

"You want me to evacuate?"

"If necessary, yes. Maria will be waiting outside; Grailly's currently by the piazza." He spoke of Jamal Iqbal. "Take the Deputy PM out to Maria, along with his wife. Minimise the threat; Special Branch can deal with the rest."

"What about the Foreign Secretary?"

"You just worry about the DPM. Edward can deal with Pickering."

"Roger that."

The stairway to the grand tier was deserted except for the same smartly dressed usher who Mike had seen on duty when he entered twenty-five minutes ago. Mike smiled at him as he climbed the stairs and turned right.

The way to Box 63.

"Evening." Mike flashed him an identity card. "I have an important message for one of your guests in Box 63. His boss was most insistent that I deliver it in person."

The attendant looked at Mike's ID. Matthew Paris. 3/4/88. Cabinet Office.

"Box 63 is along the corridor and on your left."

"Thank you."

The Bordeaux Connection

Mike passed through the doorway and followed the corridor to his right. The layout matched what he'd seen on the X-ray setting; the walls were dark red, and the artwork was primarily oil-based. The boxes were clearly marked: 60, 61 . . .

He stopped outside Box 63. As expected, the door was closed. Mike looked over his shoulder, checking his actions were unobserved. Satisfied, he decided he'd take the advice of the many. He removed the opera glasses from the case and selected the X-ray setting.

Suddenly he could see everything. The first two seats were unoccupied, while the Deputy PM and his wife sat with their backs to the doorway, their eyes solely on the stage. From where he stood, the source of the yellow light was much clearer. He estimated the shape of an ordinary drink bottle: 330ml. Approaching the door, he lowered himself down onto one knee. The bottle was standing upright below the chair. He couldn't make out the name on the label.

He rose to his feet. "Edward, we have a serious problem. We could be dealing with some form of Molotov."

Kit thought he was hearing things. The Molotov cocktail was the fancy term for an old-fashioned petrol bomb. Usually an improvised incendiary used to cause mayhem in a crowd. "You're quite sure?"

"The item is a bottle; I can't read the label. Shape looks like an ordinary Coke bottle."

Kit's eyes remained focused on the courtyard. Through the glass, he saw Everard throw his cigarette to the ground, stamp on it and remove his mobile phone.

"We need to be sure about this, Grosmont. One wrong move, and we could have a PR disaster on our hands."

"One wrong move, and we might have a terrorist attack on our hands."

"We don't know that yet. Tomorrow's papers are already going to be full of Edinburgh. The last thing we need is to give the press more to write about."

"What the hell do you suggest I do?"

Kit grimaced, anticipating the moment when Everard would return. "How close can you get?"

"Hang on a sec." He set the opera glasses to normal and lowered himself to the floor. With his face touching the ground, he placed his eye on the gap between the frame and the door. The label was Coca-Cola, the liquid black. On the face of it, it looked genuine.

"Phil, I'm guessing you can hear this? You're quite sure a fizzy drink can't account for this?"

"Only if it had some form of liquid explosive mixed in."

"You ever heard of anything like this before?"

"Not exactly. Though the IRA experimented with most things. Most likely, they're used for poisons, but without knowing who we're dealing with, it would be impossible to rule anything out. Can you reach it from where you are?"

"Possibly with the door open. Could it be booby-trapped?"

"I'd need to see a photo."

"Maybe once I'm inside. Unless you have a camera installed in these lenses."

"Sorry. Maybe next time."

Mike bit his lip. "Is Mr White with you?"

"I'm here, Grosmont." The voice was the Director's.

"I'm running out of time. I'm gonna need an answer now."

"I've told you once already. Get Hughes and his wife out of there."

"And the bottle?"

This time he paused for longer. "Leave it for the bomb squad. Just get them out. Maria will meet you on Bow Street."

"Roger that."

The Deputy PM felt a light touch on his shoulder. "Forgive the intrusion, sir, but I've been sent here by the PM. I need you to listen to me very carefully. Our intelligence has reason to believe a credible threat exists. There's a car outside waiting for you. The PM is expecting you at Number 10."

The Deputy PM twitched. Though his bearded face remained perfectly calm, Mike could tell from his body language his words had caused deep alarm. "Who are you?"

"These questions and more can be answered later. Right now, time is of the essence."

The Deputy PM turned, facing Mike head-on. Faint nearby illumination confirmed him to be a white male, late twenties, clearly of military physique.

"MI5, of course; I should have known. I'd have thought you'd all be far away. Up north. Dealing with all the mess."

Mike was happy with the incorrect guess. "The chair I'm sitting on has something very nasty situated beneath it. It could go off at any second. Carefully and slowly rise to your feet. And Mrs Hughes."

Lavinia Hughes heard every word. Despite the lack of volume in Mike's voice, each word had been uttered with clarity. She caught her husband's eye for less than a second, not daring to do the same to the stranger in the seat behind. Her husband's expression confirmed her worst fears.

We have no choice.

Placing her opera glasses in her handbag, she put the strap over her left shoulder and followed her husband towards the doorway.

Mike stood aside and quietly took in their features. Though he'd seen the Deputy PM a thousand times or more on television or in personnel shots, he was surprised at how relatively short he was in real life. At five feet nine, he was taller than many in the Cabinet, but his head barely reached Mike's mouth. His frame was also broader than Mike had previously expected. What the tailored suits hid effectively, the tuxedo exposed.

Mrs Hughes was still to acknowledge him, choosing instead to walk with her eyes on the carpet. Up close, her appearance was still attractive but different to what he'd expected. The first thing that struck him was her scent, which he immediately attributed to a luxury brand. She was smaller than her husband and thinner; he placed her at five feet five inches and under nine stone. As they headed for the stairs, she looked at him for the first time, more worried than angry. No sooner had he looked at her than she returned her attention to the ground.

She said no words.

Mike guided them to the staircase, acknowledging the usher as he passed. The Deputy PM remained silent until they began down the stairs.

"Look here, whoever you are." He kept his voice low. "I demand to know what this is really all about."

Mike answered in a similarly low tone. "Earlier this evening, we gained intelligence of a possible threat against either yourself or the Foreign Secretary," he lied. "A few minutes ago, we obtained photographic evidence of a liquid explosive beneath the seat behind you."

Hughes waited until they reached the bottom of the stairs before speaking again. "What the hell's your name?"

Mike passed him the same ID card he'd shown the usher. The Deputy PM had seen enough over the years to recognise that the signs pointed to an alias for the Security Service.

"What do I call you?"

"Your boss calls me Captain Hansen."

Returning the card to his pocket, Mike led them quietly through the lobby. On reaching the main doors, he escorted them outside onto the pavement separating the entrance from Bow Street. A blue Mercedes was waiting by the kerb; he recognised the licence plate.

"The car is for you; it'll take you both to Number 10."

"What about Richard?"

"You can leave the Foreign Secretary to me."

Mike opened the rear left door. Maria was sitting alone in the backseat, a white man in his early thirties behind the wheel. While

The Bordeaux Connection

Mike held the door open, Hughes entered tentatively. Less than a metre away, Lavinia Hughes was standing by the kerb, her face frozen with fear.

"Mrs Hughes?"

The woman delayed as her husband shuffled in alongside Maria, making room for her in the left seat. She stood with both hands glued to her handbag, her frightened eyes looking around her. The road outside the opera house was rarely deserted, but the oncoming flow of traffic was sparse. Headlights moved from her right, a black cab, its sign brightly lit.

She bolted to her right and raised her hand. "Taxi."

The cab stopped less than five metres behind the Mercedes; she had reached the rear left door by the time it had arrived. She entered in almost one fluid movement.

Immediately the taxi began to move forward.

Mike was stunned. Her movements had caught him completely cold. He closed the door on the Deputy PM and sprinted after the taxi. He saw her in the window as it passed, a look of wild terror dominating her face.

He watched it pass the stationary Mercedes and head north, away from Westminster.

Mike cursed under his breath. Through the rear windscreen of the Mercedes, he saw Maria staring at him, her words inaudible. Alongside her, the Deputy PM was pulsating with rage.

The Mercedes moved forward; he guessed on Maria's orders. As it did, Mike headed for the entrance and re-entered the foyer.

The Pit Lobby was still deserted, the occasional visitor speaking on a mobile phone or heading to the toilets the rare exception. Entering the lobby, he followed the red carpet to the doors to the concourse, where Kit had earlier seen the Foreign Secretary speaking with the man with the beard.

He spoke into his mouthpiece. "Kit, what's happening?"

Kit was standing in the same position as before. He had passed the time listening to Phil and Mr White, speaking occasionally. The cellist had finished his cigarette, but he was still to show any sign of returning to his seat. Instead, the man was concentrating on his mobile phone.

Just staring at the display.

At 19:54, the cellist checked his watch, seemingly comparing it to the display on his phone. As the seconds ticked to 19:55, he put his phone away and removed a small black object from his pocket.

Kit became immediately alarmed.

He heard Mike's voice in his right ear. Choosing to ignore him, he waited until an on-duty usher passed in the opposite direction and exited through the glass door.

The smoking section was a compact area located in the heart of Covent Garden. Night had fallen in the thirty minutes since their arrival; the external lights shone in force, creating a purple haze against the glass exterior. Thanks to the lights, the smoking section was well lit and the man's features clearly visible. Kit saw things he hadn't noticed before: a small scar on the right side of his neck and something similar on his right knuckle. His nose was more dented than he'd first realised, suggesting to Kit it had probably been broken at least once. His right cheek displayed evidence of battle scars: his left eyelid drooped slightly, definitely more so than the right. To Kit, the signs told a story. He was dealing with a seasoned operative.

A man who knew precisely what he was doing.

Mike stopped on reaching the grand staircase. His gut instinct told him to head right, the north-west side of the concourse.

"Edward, where are you?"

The question couldn't have come at a worse time.

"Don't speak again until I tell you."

Mike knew when to follow orders. Logic told him Kit was currently carrying out a stakeout, perhaps standing within earshot of his chosen target. Yet experience told him there could be a second possibility.

Kit was in trouble.

Heading to the right of the grand stairway, he followed the corridor as it wound from right to left. The concourse was still largely deserted. Most guests remained firmly in their seats as they followed the performance to the interval. Through the nearby doorways, he could hear singing, a male voice, tenor, the language unmistakably European. He glimpsed the performance on one of the monitors as he passed. An imposing man with dark hair and a beard was singing, his facial expression displaying feelings of inward torment in the stage lights.

The sound of singing came and went as he approached and passed the doors. He estimated he was nearly halfway along the right side of the building, probably close to being in line with Box 63. With the Deputy PM and his wife successfully evacuated, he guessed the box was probably still empty.

With both himself and Kit on their feet, he had no way of knowing whether the Foreign Secretary or his wife had returned.

Less than twenty metres from where the young dark-haired member of the White Hart walked the concourse in search of his colleague, the Foreign Secretary was in the pit of despair. He checked his watch; only seconds remained before the bearded cellist would carry out his threat.

And life would never again be the same.

On the floor above, the wife of the Foreign Secretary noticed the moment had come. She guessed her husband was still in the same place, doing the same as she was.

As 19:54 approached, she left the ladies and took the stairs to the ground floor. She would meet her husband in the Champagne Bar of the Paul Hamlyn Hall.

Or failing that: outside.

The Royal Opera House
19:54

Kit remained still until he was sure that Mike had got the message. He heard him reply, 'Roger that', but he didn't expand on it.

Everyone else had gone quiet, too, including Phil, who he guessed had other things on his mind. He'd heard enough over the airwaves to know that the Deputy PM was safe, a question mark remaining over his wife.

Aside from hearing cursing from both Mike and Maria, he was unsure what had become of her.

He made his way out the door, alone apart from the cellist. The man appeared to contemplate another cigarette before deciding one was enough. As he approached, he saw the black device in more detail; it was small and rectangular, with a few small buttons making up the display. Kit had seen similar things before, each time owned by explosives experts.

He assumed this was unlikely to be any different.

Less than ten metres separated them. The cellist remained with his back to the doors, his attention solely on the article in his hand. The delay was enough. Approaching from behind, Kit eased his right hand inside his jacket pocket and removed his firearm in one smooth movement.

"I wouldn't press that if I were you."

The cellist turned his head slowly, each millisecond a seemingly uncountable delay. As he did, he looked at Kit inquisitively. The scene before him was familiar, but one, somehow, he had failed to factor in. The man in front of him was tall and muscular. His fine white shirt and matching dinner jacket complemented his firm physique that reminded him of himself ten years earlier. Everything about his appearance was highly polished.

The Bordeaux Connection

There was little doubt of the man's identity.

Everard turned to face Kit, his eyes fixed in a thoughtful stare. Despite his obvious possession of a gun, Kit's actions had caused no alarm. Drawn no attention.

Instead, they remained alone.

The weapon was a Heckler & Koch USP45, a semi-automatic pistol that didn't need to be cocked. Instead, Kit kept his index finger precariously close to the trigger. He took a long intake of breath before exhaling slowly; twelve years' experience told him the best way to maintain composure was to focus on his breathing. With his arms at full stretch, he was in complete control. The barrel of the gun was pointed squarely at the cellist's chest; he had no plans for that to change. With the silencer fitted, the chances of a gunshot being heard would be minimal. The more significant problem was the size of the venue.

He guessed he had a window of no more than thirty seconds before somebody saw them.

"No sudden movements. Unless you want them to be your last."

The cellist stood perfectly still. As the seconds passed, a noise began reverberating from his pocket: music, Dvořák.

Slowly, he gestured to his pocket. "The call is from my boss. He will be most displeased if I do not answer."

Kit's face developed into a smile. "I once had a relative who used the exact same piece. Only he used it as an alarm clock."

The cellist smiled, checked his pocket and saw the display of his phone flashing the alarm setting. It was 19:55, and the button on the object in his other hand was still to be pressed.

"Hands still. You may keep hold of the phone. At least that way, I can see what you're doing." Kit moved towards him, his steps slow and composed, his eyes focused with steely concentration. "You know, I heard the exact same piece being played earlier today. It was just up the road from here, in fact. I don't suppose that was you by any chance?"

"Who are you?"

"That's hardly your concern. Nor how it is I know. What should concern you, however, is the fact that we do. Don't worry. The Deputy Prime Minister and his good lady have already vacated the premises. I'm sure his right honourable friend won't be far behind. Assuming his wife is over the bad case of mussels, of course."

The cellist again stared hard at Kit, raising his eyebrows slightly. "You're MI5?"

"If it makes you happy. I suppose I don't really need to ask who you are. Where's Randek?"

The man's expression hardened, his furrowed brow causing the lines on his forehead to thicken. He licked his lips and raised the detonator in his free hand.

"This device is capable of much. It has the power to do great harm."

"I've told you already your target has already been safely escorted from the building. The box is presently empty."

The man appeared confused. "You honestly believe that is why I'm here – one man. If I wanted to kill a member of the Cabinet, I should have done so already. On the street, in his home, this morning . . . it matters not. Should my finger accidentally slip, it is not only the box in question that is in danger, I assure you."

"Keep still," Kit said, edging closer, his arms showing no sign of fatigue. "Palms up. There's a good fellow."

The cellist rolled his shoulders and looked around. Although the noises of the city were competing with the singing from the auditorium, the secluded smokers' area was comparatively quiet and deserted, close to the opera house. "It is cold out tonight. My joints are beginning to feel chilly. Perhaps it would be nicer if we could go someplace warmer. Alone."

"Better yet, why don't you hand over your toys and return to your seat to enjoy the rest of the performance? Then again, from what I heard earlier today, you already know it by heart."

"A quite marvellous piece, we can both agree, but tonight's performance does not rank among the best. It is the same whenever such classics are brought to England. If the great man were alive today, I'll wager his work would never be seen outside the Czech Republic."

"Enough garbage!" Kit snarled. "It won't wash. Like you say, it's rather chilly out. Quite slowly, I want you to lower yourself to the ground and place both objects down. You understand?"

"The button, *Monsieur*, is very sensitive. One bad step and the repercussions could be great."

"Then, for your sake, I suggest you do it very carefully!"

Mike checked inside every doorway, inspecting the aisles for any sign of Kit. The bearded tenor was still on stage, but the limelight had fallen on a pretty young woman with a divine singing voice.

There were more people about than before. The refreshment areas didn't open till the interval; those out of their seats were mainly men heading for the toilets. Their clothing varied considerably, though the last thing Mike had expected was jeans and trainers. The age range was equally varied, from early twenties to something much more.

As he approached the bottom of the concourse, he saw an area of glass ahead, a doorway leading onto a small private courtyard. Beyond it, standing outside, were two men engaged in animated conversation.

The cellist hadn't moved for almost five seconds. His whole body, including the hand that held the device, had remained unnaturally still. His face was rigid, his eyes glazed over in a fixed stare.

Kit bit his lip and inwardly swore at the man. Though the entire episode had been of the briefest possible duration, the sight of him holding the black rectangular device had already changed from troubling to just plain irritating. The worrying thought entered Kit's mind that the person in front of him – an explosives expert, culture connoisseur and, apparently, an extremely talented musician – had an ulterior motive. If the attack on Box 63 wasn't merely about taking out the Deputy PM, over two thousand other lives could be in grave danger.

A torrent of thoughts rushed through his mind, one of which came straight to the front. Mr White had posed the question the day he joined the White Hart. What was the primary motive of terrorism?

Answer: to spread terror.

"Enough games," Kit said, brushing beads of sweat from his forehead. Though the temperature outside was cold, his body temperature was rising rapidly. "I've asked you once politely; now I really must insist. Place the object on the floor, or you leave me no alternative but to shoot you."

The cellist smiled. "You call yourself MI5? A true servant of Her Majesty the Queen would not be so reckless in his assumptions. As I tell you already, the button is sensitive. Should my hand be forced to the floor, the button will be pressed anyway. That way, we both lose."

Damn you to hell, Kit cursed in his mind. In truth, from what he could see of the design of the device, he was unsure whether that was true or not. Either way, he knew it was too big a risk to take.

"Do as I say, and you leave here alive. No dramas. Tell us about Randek, and you might even be offered immunity. One false move and rest assured: I will kill you. Unlike you, I already have that immunity."

The cellist stared unflinchingly. "Kill me here, and your chances of leaving unobserved are lost, so perhaps instead you might satisfy my curiosity. Shoot me now. Or call the police."

Kit bit his lip, his upper teeth pressing deeply into his lower gum. He tried to read the man's expression: stern, stubborn, otherwise emotionless, his blinking eyes the only movement. He knew that each second increased their chances of being observed. *Is that a good thing or a bad thing?* he asked himself. *Bad, probably*, he concluded. He held a specially authorised gun, the sight or sound of which could rapidly create panic or mass hysteria in the large, crowded venue.

A scream. Close by. Or was it?

No. Further away.

Kit's heart skipped a beat. His initial assumption was that someone had observed them.

His fears were dispelled. The sound was pre-planned; it came from the stage, singing: loud and piercing.

For a split second, he'd lost concentration; less than a second, no longer. A split second was enough. The cellist seized the moment; despite the man's bulky size, he moved quickly, his long legs creating a powerful jump.

Kit crashed down on the concrete. He felt the impact on his lower back, then the base of his skull. Everard had landed on top of him. Their faces touched. He felt sweat, strength, hair, a tickly sensation, accompanied by two forms of stench: something meat based and some form of liquor. He felt two hands pressing down firmly on each of his shoulders and a knee into his left thigh. Looking up from the ground, one sight monopolised his view: a bearded face, aggression piercing from two brown eyes. Pain shot all along his left leg, extending to his lower back.

Then he felt restriction to his neck.

The sounds of the opera still resonated loudly through the nearby doorways, the booming voice of the man with the beard replaced by that of the petite woman.

Despite the loud singing, a second noise came through equally clear from the bottom of the concourse, followed immediately by shouts of pain.

Mike saw the whole thing. He sprinted along the concourse towards the electronic doors that led out onto the smokers' section. He focused on the scene behind the glass and paused by the door, stunned.

Two men were engaged in a wrestling match.

He couldn't tell to begin with whether the man on the floor was Kit or not. All he could see was a bearded man dressed in an expensive tuxedo overpowering a similarly dressed man of a far slimmer build.

Whoever the thinner man was, he was clearly losing.

Had Mike had time to think, his reactions might have been very different. A year in the White Hart, and he was still to see Kit lose. Had he not been inches from defeat, Mike knew Kit would have resented the help.

Knowing Kit, he probably would anyway.

The man's thumbs were stubby, just like the rest of his hands. Kit estimated his total weight to be between fourteen and fifteen stone, giving him at least a two-stone advantage.

The pain throbbed in his throat, the restriction making breathing difficult. He felt an involuntary gag reflex kick in, his lungs heaving desperately for air. He grabbed the cellist's hands, focusing all his strength on pulling them from his throat. Even with a firm grip, he failed to move them.

His following action was instinctive. As his lungs began to burn, his throat on the point of closing, he knew it was time for the ultimate plan B. He'd learned that one before the White Hart, before the military. At school, in films, *Dad's Army*.

He grabbed the man's scrotum and squeezed.

The cellist screamed, loud and shrill; even with his throat constricted, Kit couldn't believe a sound that loud could go unheard. Again a split second was enough; the man's hands loosened, allowing him to roll free. Out of the corner of his eye, Kit saw his gun lying on the floor no more than five metres away. Desperately he scrambled, rolled and pointed.

The cellist had spun away in the opposite direction, giving him breathing space. As Kit went for the trigger, another sound filled his ears.

One easily loud enough to be heard elsewhere.

The Royal Opera House
19:59

The explosion happened in stages.

The pressing of the button on the remote control activated a chain reaction inside the bottle, causing the liquid to fizz. Once it did, the next stage took less than a second.

The highly flammable liquid combusted, creating an instant blast.

The people in the second tier were the first to notice something was wrong. A series of tremors preceded the blast, causing cracks in the floor and walls of the balcony boxes. As the impact faded, debris erupted from the grand tier.

Covering at least a quarter of the spectators in the orchestra stalls.

The explosion had been momentarily deafening. Even on the stage, the blast had been impossible to miss. A cloud of dust rose from the epicentre, still rising over ten seconds later. Strangely there was no smoke nor any other sign of fire beyond the initial spark of illumination. The impact had centred on Box 63, with further damage in Boxes 62 and 64. The worst area to be hit was directly below Box 63.

A stunned silence ensued. The music had stopped. People from all parts of the auditorium rose to their feet, eyes anxiously fixed on the area behind the cloud. As the dust began to settle, the extent of the destruction was revealed for the first time. A gaping hole extended into the boxes on either side of Box 63 and much of the tier below. Its former foundations now lay in heaps of rubble around the frightened crowd on the floor, dust covering their clothes and faces. The people who had sat further away had endured a narrow escape. For those located below and in the adjoining boxes, it was a different story.

Even from the amphitheatre, it was clear that the death toll would be well into double figures.

Mike felt the impact before he heard it. Though the explosion had clearly come from the floor above, even below his feet, there were shock waves.

He hit the ground immediately. The dive had been subconscious, just like the roll that followed it. Five years as a Red Beret had taught him everything he needed to know about landing properly when dropped by parachute; eighteen months since his last practice, the knowledge was still there, instinctive.

As he raised his head, he heard gasps of horror coming from nearby, a stampede of pounding feet replacing the sound of singing.

The next thing he saw was movement of a different kind. Kit was lying on his back, gun at the ready. He saw him pull the trigger, the lack of noise indicating he had fitted a silencer.

Mike rolled again, this time in the other direction, shielding his head with his hands. The nearby window had shattered; glass rained down like hail.

Kit was still on his back, apparently incapable of getting to his feet. It was obvious from his face he had sustained a powerful impact injury. His bullets had missed the cellist by inches, the last skimming the top of the man's forehead before passing through the broken glass.

Mike got to his feet, faced with two choices:

The assailant or his friend.

Kit fired until he clicked on empty and shouted, "Follow that piece of filth."

The destruction of the glass had helped the cellist make his decision. Rather than head for the piazza, taking him south-west through the heart of Covent Garden, he headed back inside the opera house and joined the mass exodus heading for Bow Street.

The Bordeaux Connection

Mike didn't look back. Even if Kit was seriously injured, he knew he'd made the correct call. Camaraderie was hugely important in the White Hart.

But the defence of the realm was always the greatest priority.

He chased the cellist through the west concourse, his legs accelerating through the gears. The cellist was moving surprisingly quickly, his destination the lobby.

A strange choice, Mike thought.

As the seconds passed, the decision suddenly made sense. Hordes of people emerged from the nearby doorways, crowding the concourse from wall to wall. People moved as if barefooted on acid, hastily heading for the main doors. He caught a view through one of the doorways of a slowly dissipating cloud of debris hanging in the air. Beyond that was the hurriedly deserted stage, curtains open and still set up for the opera. People were leaving in a panic, worried expressions confirming everyone was thinking the same thing.

It was everyone for themselves.

Mike sprinted along the concourse until the densely milling crowds forced him to reduce his pace abruptly. Not for the first time that evening, he failed to stop in time and bumped into a bystander, a casually dressed man holding his girlfriend's hand.

The cellist's head start had made the difference. As Mike approached the lobby, he saw him heading for the main doors, moving, incredibly, as though he was leaving as one of the crowd. He even stopped to help a panicked blonde lady to her feet before continuing into the foyer.

Mike focused solely on his target. With the crowds at their thickest, the man was hidden apart from the top of his head. The cellist had acted tactically and headed for an area of suited men. Mike was in danger of losing him. Jumping gave him a better view, enough to see the cellist fast approaching the main doors. The gap between them was over ten metres, and soon it would become more.

As the cellist made his way through the main door, he disappeared into the cold Bow Street air.

Kit was still lying on his back, an agonising pain in the base of his spine but otherwise uninjured.

The area around the smokers' section was still deserted. He couldn't believe so long could pass without attention being drawn to the broken glass. Even inside the concourse, evidence of his stray bullets was clear; one had caught a wall lamp and penetrated the surrounding exterior.

He grimaced as he sat up. Along the concourse, the pandemonium showed no signs of abating. People were still leaving the auditorium, the majority heading for the lobby. They moved as if oblivious to what surrounded them: as if some form of invisible beam was guiding them in one direction. Amidst the screams and shouts, he thought he heard something more direct.

Someone was speaking instructions through the PA system.

Nobody seemed to be listening.

He leaned his weight against his hands and struggled upwards. Once on his feet, he headed towards the broken window and stopped, deciding against returning inside.

He spoke into his mouthpiece. "Come in, whoever's there. What the hell's happening?"

"Where the hell are you?"

He recognised Maria's voice. "Same place. Everard set the bomb off. The whole place is a war zone."

Maria cursed under her breath. "What in God's name happened?"

"Everard had a remote detonator; it set off a liquid explosive. Pickering must have planned this all along."

"You couldn't stop it?"

"Obviously not!"

"News of an explosion is already making the news. The Director is having kittens, and the PM is currently on the phone.

I'm heading there now, and I'm going to need something to tell him."

Kit took a deep breath, attempting to remain calm. "Everard wasn't interested in the DPM. That was just a by-product. He wasn't interested even when I tried to tell him the box was empty. The plan was to proceed anyway."

"How many casualties?"

"I don't know; I haven't seen the wreckage. Judging by the sound, I think we'll be lucky to escape with less than double figures."

Another curse. "Where the hell's Everard?"

"On the run. Grosmont left with him."

"Let's hope to God he catches him. Where are you?"

"Near the concourse. I'm injured. I can't run."

"Can you walk?"

"Yes."

"You go after Pickering. I'll send someone else for his wife."

The onrush had dwindled by the time Kit finally got inside. Stepping over the remains of the recently annihilated window, he jogged in anguish back along the west concourse and headed left through an open doorway.

He'd last seen the Foreign Secretary entering the toilets almost ten minutes earlier. Logic told him the man would have moved on by now, most likely departing unseen amongst the masses. If all went according to protocol, a special order would have been placed to ensure all Members of Office were accounted for.

As far as Kit was aware, no such order had been made.

He entered the gents and looked in every direction. The facilities had suffered damage: a broken mirror hung from the wall above the sinks, its remains scattered across the floor. A pipe had exploded, causing water to pool; the lights, however, were still working, reflecting off what remained of the mirrors. Unsurprisingly the urinals were vacant, as were most of the cubicles.

One appeared to be locked.

Kit approached the locked cubicle and knocked gently on the door. "Mr Pickering. Sir, my name is Masterson. I've been sent by the Cabinet Office to escort you back to Whitehall. There's a car waiting close by."

He waited, hearing nothing.

"Sir, if you can hear me, we must move fast. The traffic outside is already gridlocked; the PM has demanded your safe return. The crowds have gone; the building is empty."

He heard movement from within, the lock sliding to one side.

The reverberations from the explosion had been frightening, even compared to what he'd prepared for. Being on the west side of the opera house, experiencing the damage first-hand had been unavoidable. He'd heard what sounded like a mirror falling, followed by running water that quickly flowed beneath the cubicle door, soaking the bottom of his shoes. As the seconds passed, the sound of nearby chaos became overwhelming. People were fleeing in terror, worried observers desperately trying to ensure loved ones got out safely.

Tentatively, Pickering opened the door. The man in front of him was dark-haired and sharply dressed. His stature and voice carried clear authority.

Kit addressed him. "Are you okay? Have you sustained injuries?"

"No. Just a slightly upset stomach." He looked around, noticing that the source of the running water was a burst pipe slowly flooding the room.

Kit, meanwhile, took a step back, taking in the man's features. As before, an elegant tuxedo and spotless white shirt fitted tightly to his medium build, a blue bow tie endorsing his political allegiance. The man's face was pale, his cheeks flushed; unlike earlier that evening, his appearance was ragged.

The man looked as though he'd seen a ghost.

"Sir . . ."

The Bordeaux Connection

"My wife?"

Kit pressed his earpiece. "Maria, I need an update on the Foreign Secretary's wife."

"I'm sending someone to take care of her."

Kit looked at Pickering. "She's safe."

Outside the main façade on Bow Street, the wife of the Foreign Secretary heard someone call her name. The voice had a clear feminine pitch, yet its tone was far more authoritative than she was used to dealing with.

The woman was blonde, her long hair tied back in a ponytail. Her expression was warm but no-nonsense. A woman under orders from the very top.

"Mrs Pickering, I'm with the Cabinet Office. I'm under strict orders to take you home."

"My husband?"

"Your husband is being evacuated as we speak. We have a car waiting for you."

Mrs Pickering looked at the woman and smiled tentatively. She wiped fresh tears from her eyes and proceeded cautiously through the rapidly increasing crowd.

In less than three minutes, the capacity-filled venue had been completely vacated. With the auditorium empty, the full-strength overhead lights and the recently used props on the stage were a strange combination; one the Foreign Secretary never believed he'd see.

Against Kit's wishes, Pickering had entered the stalls through one of the doorways.

As he looked up at Box 63, the damage was revealed for the first time. A crimson-coloured void had appeared between Boxes 62 and 64. It was as though a bottomless hole had swallowed everything within a ten-metre circumference. The whole tier on that side had become unstable; he feared even a heavy footstep would cause it to cave in.

Holding his breath, he felt the hand of his rescuer guide him towards the doorway. Turning, he headed for the deserted exit onto the piazza.

The Royal Opera House
20:03

The area outside the grand façade was crowded. In Everard's experience, leaving such venues was essentially the same after every performance, be it at Covent Garden, Drury Lane, Edinburgh, Paris, Moscow or Madrid. The bigger the platform, the more likely the delays.

Today he was experiencing the worst.

The grand entrance led directly onto Bow Street, a short step from the pavement. Like most in that part of the city, the road was dual lane but narrow, with traffic building up from both directions. Several parking bays were fully occupied on the opposite side of the street, forcing new arrivals to find a space along the nearby kerb, ignoring the double yellow lines. Further along Wellington Street, he saw flashing blue lights, accompanied by a fire engine's siren. In the distance, he heard a similar sound, almost certainly an ambulance.

With the traffic as it was, he guessed they would have a long wait.

The pavement was overcrowded, particularly around the main entrance. The same was true outside the Paul Hamlyn Hall, which adjoined the main theatre to the south-east. Through the glass exterior, he could see more people still coming out, entering the area around the champagne bar down the staircases connected to the upstairs restaurant or from the concourse outside the auditorium.

The cellist knew he had only two reasonable options. North-west or south-east. North-west would take him to the top of Bow Street, giving him the second choice of continuing to Endell Street or left to the Underground station at Covent Garden. South-east would take him towards the river, across the Strand and Waterloo

Bridge. At the Strand, he would have two further choices, left or right.

Westminster or not Westminster.

He chose right, south-east along Bow Street, his destination, the Strand. The sirens were getting louder, the sight of a large fire engine in front of him revving urgently as it sought to approach the opera house. Keeping close to a large crowd, he used a zebra crossing where Bow Street met Russell Street and continued with the plan. He looked over his shoulder for the first time since he left the building, wondering if either of his dark-haired pursuers had made it out. Sure enough, one of them was on the pavement, scanning the crowds purposefully. Their eyes met from across the street; he detected a distinct change in the man's body language.

Quickly he turned away, upping his pace as he moved through the unsuspecting crowds.

Mike had finally made it out. The crowds moved even slower close to the doors; members of staff were shouting at length, requesting calm.

The requests were still falling on deaf ears.

Mike wanted to punch someone. He'd witnessed the culprit detonate the bomb and, somehow, make it unobserved to the main exit. As a kid, his uncle had once told him of Sod's Law: if something can go wrong, it will happen – and always at the worst possible time. As he neared the doors, the only thing that stood in his way were the people he'd tried to save, pushing and shoving in every direction. As he reached the doorway, the people in front of him stopped, threatening a scrum. He heard Kit shout something in his earpiece about nailing the bastard.

Sod it!

He solved his problem with one swift push. He saw a man and a woman fall to the floor – *that'll teach the idiots for blocking the doorway to a bomb scene!* It created a gap wide enough for him to make it outside, along with five other lucky people.

The Bordeaux Connection

The first thing he noticed was how loud it was. Flashing lights appeared to his right. A fire engine stopped at the crossroads where Jay had earlier dropped him off. People had gathered on the road and were blocking the path to the opera house.

Sod's Law's at it again.

The cellist had at least ten seconds on him; more than enough, he feared, for a man who knew what he was doing. Among the masses, individuals were difficult to pick out; the flashing blue lights distorted their features that were already hard to see in the poor light.

Seeing nothing to his left, he headed right, south-east. Further along the road, the people were more spread out. A second siren was approaching, and a police motorcycle appeared alongside the fire engine, its driver choosing the pavement as a better alternative to driving on a gridlocked road. The man lifted his visor and barked orders for people to get out of the way, causing unsuspecting bystanders to lurch in terror.

Mike saw him coming. He grabbed a couple on the kerb, who were unaware of the approaching danger, and held them until the bike had passed. Deciding against waiting for any words of thanks, he burst into a jog towards Russell Street and stopped on reaching the crossroads.

Some of the onlookers had decided enough was enough. A large group, comprised mostly of couples, with clothing ranging from casual to opulent, crossed the road before heading either south or east. He saw someone matching Everard's appearance weaving his way in and out of the gaps. Seconds later, his suspicions were confirmed. As Everard turned, he caught sight of him face on, his wary eyes peering back.

Mike stood on the side of the road, feeling suddenly numb. He wanted to move, but his body was frozen as if the man's eyes had placed him in a hypnotic trance. The delay lasted seconds, though it felt more like minutes; time no longer seemed to register clearly. On both sides of the road, the crowds continued to move. Everard was the only exception; instead, he stared back, his large brown eyes giving off an aura of total concentration.

Mike felt a bump from his right, returning him to reality. A Japanese man apologised to him before immediately walking on alongside his girlfriend. A police car passed the crossing, obscuring his view. When it had passed, Everard had disappeared.

Running south-east.

"Hey!"

Mike sprinted over the zebra crossing. The traffic was moving more steadily now. Though he missed the police car, he only narrowly avoided crashing into a second fire engine, receiving a honk from the driver.

He shouted again at Everard, this time drawing attention from passing bystanders. Some among the crowds came to a stop, allowing him space to burst into a full sprint.

The bump from the Japanese man had done him good. He was thinking again, quickly and sensibly. The best chance he had of stopping him was to make him a target. That meant shouting.

"Hey! Stop that man. You with the beard! Hey!"

The shouts successfully created attention, less so in getting anyone to comply. If anything, the louder he shouted, the more people stepped out of the way.

He re-established visual contact midway along Wellington Street. Most of the outlets were closing while the restaurants were approaching their busy period. A large white van was parked outside a closed bar and grill between Café Rouge and the Bella Italia. The pavements were still crowded but far less than outside the opera house. People walked the street in both directions, some coming in and out of the various wineries and eateries. Their general appearances had changed; he was over three hundred metres from the opera house, far enough, it seemed, to reintegrate with the rest of the city. Despite further arrivals from the emergency services, their approach heralded by the deafening wailings of sirens, the people's expressions suggested confusion as much as panic. A quick look over his shoulder confirmed there was no evidence of fire from the outside.

Nor did he expect it.

Wellington Street curved south-east and ended at a pedestrian island close to the Strand. Mike anticipated a left turn as Everard crossed Tavistock Street between the Bella Italia and a coffee house, but the Frenchman continued straight over.

Mike increased his pace, looking both ways as he approached Tavistock Street. One-way signs were prevalent. He chanced to cross with a car turning left off Wellington Street, causing it to skid to a halt; horns blared out indignantly. The same pattern continued on Wellington Street: Everard weaving in and out of approaching bystanders, passing the various establishments.

A hundred metres on, Mike made out another possible left turn, Exeter Street. Again, Everard made the same move, faking a turn to the left before heading towards the bottom of Wellington Street. Like the previous turn, the street was one-way, but in the opposite direction; a stationary car waiting to emerge was the only possible deterrent. Safely across, he followed the road as it curved to its end at an island where punters at the Wellington Pub stood drinking outside under the bright glare of external lights. He saw Everard run between a bike rack and a red telephone box, heading for the side of the road. He stopped in front of another zebra crossing.

Then he changed direction and headed left.

Getting the Foreign Secretary out unseen was easier than Kit had imagined. Taking advantage of the time lag between the mass exodus and convincing the Foreign Secretary to leave the gents, he led the politician around the deserted concourse. They headed through a less crowded part of the opera house to a revolving door that ran out onto the piazza.

He heard a horn, courtesy of Jay, from a car parked on double yellow lines at the end of Russell Street.

Kit ushered the Foreign Secretary into the back seat and closed the door behind him.

"Right, time to talk. What in God's name have you got yourself involved in?"

The Foreign Secretary's facial expression changed in an instant. Instead of seeing his wife and preparing to be chauffeured to the Cabinet Office, he found himself alongside the well-dressed man with dark-rimmed spectacles and an Asian driver of equally impressive features.

"I beg your pardon!"

"You can dispense with the diversion, Foreign Secretary. That kind of thing has never washed with me. I know you're involved in tonight's unfortunate business, and I need some answers – now!"

The Foreign Secretary was fuming. "How dare you. When I find out who you are, I assure you you'll be entering the next stage of your career on a laundry frigate. Do you seriously not know who I am?"

"Sadly, I know exactly who you are, which makes this whole mess all the more ghastly." Kit removed his mobile phone from his pocket, unlocked the keypad and browsed the photo gallery.

"You'll recognise this man, of course," Kit said, showing him the image on the screen. As the middle-aged politician's green eyes took in the scene, Kit could see his expression change from fury to bewilderment. "He's on our database under many names – I understand you know him best as Everard Payet." Kit scrolled through the images he'd taken earlier that night, ending with a clear shot of the politician's face. "You'll recognise this man, too, I should imagine?"

The Foreign Secretary's face had reddened considerably. "What the hell have you done with my wife?"

"She's safe; you can rely on that. Right now, I'd guess one of my colleagues is currently having the same chat with her as we are now. Assuming, of course, she's recovered from the bad mussels."

"You arrogant bastard. You're all the same in MI5, aren't you? It's something about the Oxbridge education that just turns you all into self-absorbed egotistical pricks!" He waved his finger. "I'll have your tie for this."

Kit put away his phone and removed his glasses. "Foreign Secretary, we can do this the easy way or the hard. The man with whom I photographed you in conversation, not ten minutes before the explosion that has killed at least a dozen innocent people, was witnessed by no less than two members of my organisation putting his finger to the damn button. He's currently at large in the city, and the last I saw being pursued at speed by one of my colleagues. Even if I overlook the fact that his name is already known to us and that the man is also wanted in connection with three criminal acts connected to a well-known terrorist gang, he also personally ties you to this attack and those who commanded it."

He moved closer, their faces inches apart. "Think hard, Foreign Secretary. Right now, you're looking at life in prison and one heck of a lot of front-page headlines. Who put you up to this?"

"I'm not speaking to anyone before I see my solicitor."

"A terrorist is currently at large in Britain's capital city, and for all I know, he's capable of doing the same again. Speak now, and further lives might be spared."

"I told you before, I'm not speaking to anybody before I've consulted my solicitor."

Downing Street appeared the same as usual; at least, that was the view from the gate. A smartly dressed security guard saluted on inspecting the driver's ID before allowing him access to Number 10.

Maria left the car and held the door open for the Deputy Prime Minister. She smiled at him humourlessly.

"The PM is waiting for you inside."

The man smiled awkwardly, his beard thickening as if he'd just been injected with a syringe. As Hughes disappeared inside, Maria returned to the car.

"The queen has safely returned to the castle," she spoke into her headset.

"Well, at least that's something."

She realised she was speaking to Mr White. "What news on the bishop?"

"His wife is safely under our protection. We're still awaiting word on her husband."

Maria was relieved. "And the queen's wife?"

"Nothing. The taxi was black, with a lit display. Apparently, Grosmont saw the registration and passed it on to Phil."

"Any leads on the destination?"

"Ducked out on reaching Leicester Square."

"She took the Underground?"

"According to the driver, she was last seen heading in that direction; after giving him a very generous tip."

"Maybe she'll show up on CCTV."

"Enquiries are ongoing. Sadly, you know better than most just what these things are like."

"Any news on the suspect?"

"Not a word. All attempts to contact Grosmont and Edward have failed. Though apparently, Grailly has had contact with Edward."

"Most likely a sign that they're busy doing their job."

"We'd better hope so. All I know is that at least twelve people have lost their lives, and one of my agents obtained visual evidence connecting the Foreign Secretary with the whole affair. The news channels are already giving the explosion extensive coverage. It's only a matter of time before the tabloids start asking questions."

"Any word from the PM?"

"No, but rest assured, I'm expecting it."

"Where do you want me now?"

"The knights are to hold council at the Rook at 20:15 hours. Be there when it begins."

"Yes, sir."

She tapped the side of her earpiece and told the driver, "The Old Admiralty Building. I've only got ten minutes."

The Bordeaux Connection

Oblivious to the recent scare in Covent Garden, the blonde woman in her early fifties alighted the Underground at London Bridge and moved quickly through the main concourse. She bought a ticket at the first free machine she found using cash. Doing her best to avoid detection from the overhead security cameras, she followed the signs for platform one.

The Strand
20:09

The cellist's decision to change direction seemed illogical to Mike for several reasons. On the one hand, it allowed Everard to continue running without stopping or crossing busy streets, but it also took him east onto the Strand.

Renowned for being one of the most crowded areas in London.

Predictably, the roads were jammed. The sight of the red-top buses crawling in both directions was as common as the sound of revving engines. The pavements were busy on both sides. People made their way south-west past Savoy Street in the direction of Trafalgar Square or north-east past King's College and Somerset House to the Inns of Court and Blackfriars. Though it was crowded, Mike had known it far busier. It was after eight, and the shops were in the process of closing, their previously illuminated interiors hidden by metallic shutters. As people gathered around the pubs and the takeaways, the smell of coffee, beer, chips, burgers and kebabs created a strange aroma as they merged with the exhaust fumes of the slow-moving traffic.

Staying on the north side, Everard narrowly avoided getting hit by passing cars as he crossed the intersection where the Strand joined Aldwych. Mike followed less than fifteen metres behind, on this occasion managing to time his crossing to perfection. Everard's decision was working out well. Crossing busy roads was always a lottery; a wrong decision could result in serious injury or loss of life. On the flip side, an aptly-timed unexpected turn could provide the perfect moment of camouflage. Everard had tried it twice already; Mike guessed it would only be a matter of time before he did so again. Quietly, he was impressed by the man's stamina. He didn't look like an athlete; if he had served in the forces, his appearance had deteriorated faster than his fitness. Mike calculated he would win the race over the distance.

The key was to keep him in sight.

Everard kept close to the greenery on the left side, away from the main road. Interestingly, it was where he was receiving the least resistance – as if people were purposely staying out of his way. Mike shouted in his direction, but after achieving nothing, he decided to change tactics. The age of the camera phone was making his life harder; he remembered Kit had once speculated what James Bond would have done if asked for a selfie. The times were changing; the transition would continue. In a perfect world, people would just leave them to it – no dramas, no attention.

He was amazed they'd made it so far without attracting attention.

The cellist had made it this far; for that, he was thankful. His heart was pounding like a jackhammer.

He knew he wasn't out of the woods yet.

The Strand was never the easiest part of London to negotiate, particularly when one was a wanted murderer. Thanks to the closure of the station at Aldwych, escape options were more limited than they used to be.

Such factors could often be critical.

Experience told him he had made the correct decision. Even if his pursuer was an expert on the ins and outs of the city, he doubted the man's knowledge would be greater than his. As he reached a point opposite the concrete façade of King's College, he knew he would be faced with another important decision. The A4 was a unique road, partly because of the layout. Less than one hundred metres in front of him, the church of St Mary le Strand loomed over him like a miniature St Paul's. Its extravagant baroque ornamentation was a picture under the bright floodlights. The church was also unique; aside from its famed connection with the Women's Royal Naval Service, it was located on a traffic island.

Again, two choices. Left and around. Or right to the church.

Mike thought he was seeing things. The subject was proving easy enough to track but impossible to predict.

A right turn across the road to the south side of the Strand was a manoeuvre that required a great deal of skill. To play the percentages, it was not something to be tried in one go, at least when the traffic was moving. A more sensible ploy would be to cross the road in stages.

Beginning with the traffic island outside the church.

Stage one didn't surprise him; Mike reasoned he'd have done the same thing had the shoe been on the other foot.

What happened next was far more unexpected.

Instead of circling the outer walls to the right, he headed straight between the open gates and entered the church.

The church was usually locked by now; the signs by the door confirmed that 4 p.m. was the routine closing time on weekdays. Today, however, was different.

A special service of thanksgiving was being conducted.

The cellist slowed his pace on reaching the main door and quietly headed inside. He bowed his head and closed the second door behind him before drifting towards the left side of the church.

Mike had no choice but to follow him. Raising the latch, he pushed firmly against the first door, doing his best to avoid the inevitable prolonged creak as it opened and closed. The first thing that struck him was the smell: a powerful incense that caught him by surprise. Even from the back of the church, he could tell that a service was in progress, the mellow tunefulness of the music and singing amplified by the acoustic properties of the grandiose architecture.

He entered through a second glass door and looked around at the ornate interior, an impressive assortment of a plastered gold and white ceiling and walls that reminded him of Michelangelo.

The Bordeaux Connection

The congregation was small, most occupying the front three pews on either side of a red and blue tiled aisle and kneeling on cushioned kneelers adorned with a picture of an anchor. Though of a Catholic upbringing, Mike knew enough about the Anglican order of service to recognise that the service was one of remembrance.

It was unusual for visitors to arrive this late.

Standing near the last pew, he surveyed everything in front of him. There were no side chapels, no elaborate archways. Unlike the great cathedrals he'd visited throughout his life, there were no obvious secrets or escape routes. If Everard were to leave, he'd have to do so the same way he arrived.

The cellist had experience on his side; he kept reminding himself of the fact. A stranger entering the church for the first time, their attention taken by the elaborate architecture, would be lulled into a false sense of perspective. *Churches often have a habit of doing that*, he mused, especially in Europe; a doorway or stairway heading in one direction could easily be mistaken for going somewhere else.

The arrival of his pursuer was unlikely to take long. Sure enough, less than ten seconds passed before he heard the extended creaking of the ancient door, moving both ways on its hinges. For the first time, he allowed himself a long look at the man's features. He placed him at around six-one, his strong dark brown hair in a well-cut short style that seemed to be both loved by women and approved by the military. Like the man he'd tangled with earlier, he was handsome, though without the superficial arrogance. There was something different about this one; he was younger, yes, but also more respectful – a man who had perhaps been brought up with a good understanding of humility. There had been no silver spoon in his upbringing, no wasted Eton or Harrow education, no double coloured lines or boarding. In another time and place, he knew he could almost have learned to respect him.

As the door closed, he saw his pursuer enter slowly, his eyes immediately falling on the area before the altar where the most prominent members of the congregation were gathered. He saw someone look around, a black man in his fifties. Unlike the newcomer, he felt sure that no one had observed his own entrance. Even the vicar had been concentrating on other matters. Admittedly, the chap might have found it odd: two strangers appearing one after the other, close to the end of the service. Yet so far, neither of them had done anything to draw attention. He detected from the sombre ambience it was a private affair.

Not one to gatecrash.

The sights were what he'd expected, not that Mike was familiar with the layout. The service was in honour of a former local; the lack of attendees suggested observation was intended for the minority. There was something about how the congregation stood that implied intimacy: family, friends, distant relatives. Though all were welcome, only one attendee stood out from the crowd.

The cellist was kneeling two pews from the back.

Mike genuflected before the altar and slid in alongside the cellist. He lowered himself to his knees and joined his hands together.

"I just heard on the news that the explosion at the Royal Opera House has been labelled a terrorist attack. The PM is expected to make a statement soon." He kept his voice low, his eyes alternating between the man alongside him and the altar. "Apparently, the death toll could be well into the twenties."

The cellist maintained a calm façade. "God moves in mysterious ways."

Mike edged nearer. Despite the criminal being cornered, the last thing he wanted was for the conversation to be overheard. "Killing innocent people has nothing to do with God. Your bosses have never even claimed that." He continued to keep his voice low. "I understand the Deputy PM's wife has confessed everything. The Foreign Secretary is currently being questioned as we speak."

134

The Bordeaux Connection

The cellist bowed his head, maintaining the illusion of being in prayer. Though the man's voice sounded genuine, he sensed it was probably not.

Why tell the truth?

"It must be a very difficult time for the service. I remember the last time your organisation faced a problem of this magnitude."

"Well, it was only the day before yesterday. I'm guessing you were present in Edinburgh."

The man laughed, a low whisper. "I suppose for a man as young as you, it is difficult to recall anecdotes your predecessors might have found amusing. If your bosses failed to tell you everything, or worse, repeated lies, then it's no surprise you find yourself knowing so little about what causes such great unrest." He turned to face him, his brown eyes reflecting the light as if he were a reptile. "Always remember: the only way to be certain not to lose a fight is not to get into it in the first place."

"Perhaps you're unaware, but you are currently wanted for the murder of at least twelve people, including the attempted murder of at least one cabinet minister. The Foreign Secretary is a dangerous man. One wrong word and I'm sure it won't take much persuasion for that count to rise to two. Think hard, *Monsieur*. Act reasonably now, and you might even be granted asylum."

The cellist laughed, which confused Mike.

"You think me insincere?"

"As a young man born in England, I'm guessing you will be unfamiliar with the story of Yves de Bonaire. He was a local man from a village near where I was born, though many centuries earlier. When the Huguenots brought iconoclasm to the region, de Bonaire attacked a coach of Huguenots with gunpowder, killing twenty-four. Thanks to him, the church was saved, and he spent the next week there, safe from trouble."

"Is that why you came here – looking for sanctuary? In Nottingham, they say Robin Hood once tried the same thing."

"Ah, the noble outlaw." He looked Mike in the eye, his expression between sternness and amusement. "Sometimes, to do good, evil is necessary."

"Yes. And if you want peace, war is inevitable, very profound," Mike replied. "I must say, your actions tonight have left me slightly confused. Surely Mrs Hughes's theft from the house in Somerset means she's on your side. Or are you simply trying to limit collateral damage?"

Again, he smiled. "My friends are patient men, *Monsieur*, but they are also shrewd. In business, you can pay hundreds of thousands of euros for success and be repaid with incompetence. The future is unwritten. Chances sometimes need to be taken. Such is the way of this world. Yet, in such uncertain times, it is unwise to overplay one's hand, particularly when the odds are stacked in another's favour. Take my advice: go home to your girlfriend. Enjoy life's privileges." He gestured with his fingers. "Don't enter fights you cannot win."

"You honestly believe you're in a position to make assumptions? That your actions have been going unnoticed? It may surprise you to know that you're not the only people capable of tracing a source. If Pickering duped Hughes, Pickering's lot is already lost. If others duped Pickering, then, believe me, even if he decides to reveal little, it will still be enough to compromise your endeavour. And based on events this evening, I suspect he might take little convincing, even without the need for further threats."

"We are digressing. And the hour is late." He looked towards the altar. The hymn was over; further readings were imminent. "Whatever information you seek, even if you obtained it tonight, it would still do you little good." He moved into the pew, removed a folded piece of paper from his pocket and scribbled a short note. "Take this. Your bosses at MI5 may enjoy it as a consolation prize."

Mike took it sceptically. "You still think I'm MI5?"

The cellist looked at him and smiled. "Ah, of course. *Ich Dien. Houmout.*" He looked Mike in the eye, his withered face alive with a new sense of mystery. He crossed out what he'd written and scribbled something new. "How stupid I must have been. Take the note to your boss anyway; he might find it amusing. In fact, why not take this one too?"

The cellist removed a second piece of paper from his pocket and opened it in Mike's face. A powerful mist caught him in the eyes. He recoiled instinctively and covered his face, his eyes watering. As he fell to one side, he heard movement along the pew to his left, followed by the creaking of a door.

The Strand
20:14

The pain on his cheeks made him want to slump to the ground and scream. His face was on fire, the burning on his skin agonising. He remembered experiencing a similar sensation once before, in training, years ago – though the substance used on that occasion had been far less concentrated. Reassuringly he also recalled that the effects were said rarely to last more than ten seconds.

Sure enough, as the seconds passed, his vision quickly returned to normal. The intense stinging sensation was replaced by a strange feeling of coolness that he attributed to a fresh breeze. He rubbed his eyes and looked over his shoulder.

The main door to the church was once again open.

His mistake was unforgivable. His job had been simple. Maintain surveillance of the terrorist until help arrived. He cursed himself for falling into such an obvious trap. The delay had given the cellist at least a ten-second head start.

Mike feared it would prove decisive.

The smoke had engulfed the last four pews; even now, it still lingered. The last thing Mike saw as he left the church was an astounded vicar and a shell-shocked congregation.

He left without saying a word, hurrying towards the open door.

Experience was on the cellist's side, as it always was. Game time was the most valuable thing in the world, even compared to training. Failure would only be caused by incompetence or arrogance.

He now knew the young operative could possess nothing he hadn't already seen.

The Bordeaux Connection

The Strand had ground to a standstill, which was convenient. Taking advantage of the lack of movement, he sprinted south before continuing east past the front of King's College.

Again, he had two choices: the poor and the sensible.

In less than one hundred metres, there would be a turning on the right and, shortly after that, his escape route.

Mike had learned to follow his instincts. Trusting them in times of danger and crisis was one of the first things that Kit had told him. People had different theories of what it could achieve.

Kit put it down to simply 'Being the best'.

On the Strand, traffic moved slowly in both directions, with pedestrians obscuring the fronts of the nearby buildings. Scanning the crowds on the south side, something caught his eye. Someone was jogging; though only the top of his head was visible, he recognised it immediately.

The cellist had crossed the road and was heading east towards Fleet Street and Ludgate Hill.

Mike needed to head south. With the traffic lights green, he knew crossing the road would only be possible once they changed. Heading east, his view was good enough to keep the target in clear sight.

Visual contact, at least, had been re-established.

He heard a voice in his ear, Maria's. She'd been speaking since the smoke bomb went off; he was still to reply.

Clearly, she'd heard the whole conversation.

"Grosmont?" Her voice had grown louder.

"I'm back in pursuit. Heading east. Outside Somerset House."

He followed the cellist from the north side; as far as he could tell, Everard was still to look back. *Focus or arrogance*, he wondered. *Perhaps both.*

The main building of King's College was long and prestigious and located directly opposite St Mary's. Where the traffic island ended, almost directly opposite the north-east wing of the college, an adjoining side street headed south off the Strand, leading to Temple Place.

He saw Everard take a right, looking over his shoulder as he turned. As he did, he saw Mike standing opposite, preparing to cross.

The cellist burst into a sprint.

Jay pulled up outside the Cabinet Office, and the rear left door opened immediately. Kit got out first and addressed the Foreign Secretary, "After you."

Pickering left the car gingerly, his expression one of intense frustration. He addressed Kit as he closed the door.

"What did you say your name was again?"

"Masterson, sir."

"Masterson." He eyed Kit venomously. "Rest assured, I'll be speaking to your superior about you first thing tomorrow morning. We'll see if you're still smiling once you've swapped the suit for the scrubbing brush."

Kit waited for the Foreign Secretary to approach the main doors and spoke into his mouthpiece. "Maria, I've escorted the Foreign Secretary to the Cabinet Office building. We're just waiting for someone to let us in."

"Understood."

The doors opened as if in direct response, revealing a well-lit corridor that Kit had missed earlier that day. He repeated the words, "After you," and followed the cabinet minister inside.

Pickering had stopped just inside the main door, a deeply fearful look suddenly replacing the previous air of superiority and arrogance. Standing, with arms crossed, in the corridor beyond the door were six police officers. A smartly dressed detective stood imposingly at the front, his expression offering little sympathy. Kit saw the Foreign Secretary look at him, speechless, as the detective read him his rights before escorting him from the building.

"Enjoy the rest of your evening, sir."

The Bordeaux Connection

Mike was running out of options. Failure to cross the road could cause him to lose track of the man and compromise the mission. But crossing with the traffic moving would involve the risk of serious injury.

He waited until a black taxi passed and sprinted for the dotted line in the middle of the road. A black Ford skidded to an exaggerated halt. Seizing his chance, he continued across, heading for a side road.

The sign referred to Surrey Street, new ground. Though he knew the Strand well, this was the first time he had heard of Surrey Street. To his right, the buildings that made up King's College towered above him like scenes from Georgian England. To his left, structures of similar appearance were unknown to him. There were cars on the road, but nothing to worry about compared to the traffic on the Strand. Logic told him the cellist was heading for the river.

Either that or he was playing guessing games.

The street ended at Temple Place, at which point things began to make sense. Over fifty metres ahead, Mike saw the cellist change direction again and head towards the entrance to the Tube.

Everard could feel his body starting to tire. Sweat poured down his forehead and back, pooling in wet patches on his shirt. His feet were raw, his soles blistered, his quads and calves aching and sore.

His pursuer had pushed him to his limit.

The station at Temple was always crowded, but fortunately, he'd seen it worse. At 20:15, the peak hour had long since passed, the numbers down on what would have greeted him two hours earlier. He swiped his Oyster Card on reaching the turnstiles and headed right.

District and Circle eastbound.

As he descended the stairway, he heard footsteps echoing behind him. Mike had emerged, heading for the turnstile. He ducked his head as he saw his young pursuer scanning the crowds, possibly seeing him. Timing was now everything.

He prayed the train would be imminent.

Mike didn't have a ticket readily available. Though every White Hart operative was issued an Oyster Card, he didn't have time to search his wallet. A steady queue was forming at the turnstile; he could tell from their body language that most were seasoned career people in a hurry to get home. He estimated the wait time would be well over ten seconds.

Too long.

He shouted and removed an ID badge from his pocket, flashing it as he passed. He jumped the turnstile in one swift movement, narrowly avoiding kicking two people in the head. A piercing shout came from the nearest member of the Transport Police.

Mike ignored him and sprinted towards the eastbound stairwell. A large crowd was moving in his direction, indicating a train had just arrived. Its recent passengers made their way tenaciously up the nearby stairway to the exit.

The platform was close; he could smell the warm recycled air pushing up against him as though he'd recently entered a sauna. He took shallow breaths as he slowed his pace, trying his best to postpone the intake of lactic acid around his legs.

A train was on the platform. People entered every carriage. Everard was already there, heading for the nearest doorway as the "Please mind the gap" message played automatically through the local speakers.

Everard was successfully aboard; Mike saw him move along the carriage before losing sight of him amongst a cluster of passengers. He was closing in on the doors, closer, closer still. He heard a whistling sound followed by several bleeps.

Time was running out. He went through the gears, nearer and nearer. He saw the doors closing; surely less than a second remained. He tried to slow his pace but failed.

Losing control of his feet, he smashed into the doors and bounced backwards.

The Bordeaux Connection

Everard didn't dare look. He knew his pursuer had made it onto the platform, his pace quickening with every step.

A large group of men was standing near the carriage's rear. He moved towards them, trying to hide behind a covering of bodies. He heard bleeps coming from the doors. As the doors closed, he breathed a deep sigh of relief, allowing the recycled air to enter his lungs.

He heard a thumping sound, followed by the feeling of vibrations. Something had hit the side of the train; he looked and saw what was responsible. People watched from the windows, stunned and confused at the sight of the young man outside the doors.

As the engines roared into life, he smiled, no longer bothered by the feelings of discomfort or sweat. There was a chance he wasn't out of the woods yet, but at least he'd bought himself a moment to catch his breath.

Mike somehow managed to remain on his feet. He'd taken the impact on his arms, fortunately avoiding injury. As the train began to move, he felt the developing feeling of fury escalate as he watched the looks of surprise on the faces of the onlookers.

Amongst the passengers, he saw one with no right to be there. The cellist was on the opposite side of the carriage; he'd somehow managed to find himself a seat. As the train departed, he saw him wave, then stop.

Then look away.

He heard someone calling him from behind, the Transport Police. Slowly, he turned, looking the man in the eye.

He removed his ID card from his pocket.

Everard had never been so relieved. Ten years earlier, he knew the race would have been more straightforward, but today the unthinkable had nearly happened. There was always a chance that luck would run out one day, and everything for which life had been lived, preparations made, would simply be in vain.

Today, thankfully, was not that day.

Still, one thought continued to linger. The man had got close, too close. He'd seen two of them; had it not been for the conversation in the church, he would never have made the connection. The full repercussions would be made known and appropriate actions taken in time. The discovery was arguably as priceless as the mission itself.

After all these years, he had proof that the order still survived.

In a first-class carriage on a train heading into the east of the country, Mrs Hughes heard her mobile phone ring. Removing it from her handbag, she checked the display and saw it was from her husband, his mobile number.

There were things that needed to be said. Things that would make sense in time. *He deserves the truth,* she thought. In no circumstances would the opposite be true.

But now was not the time.

Ignoring it, she placed her phone back inside her handbag and closed her eyes.

Below the Old Admiralty Building
20:39

The meetings always started on time. Even in the darkest of scenarios, Maria had never known anything else. It was the way of the organisation, the way of the country. *How many times had similar things occurred?* she wondered as she gazed at the secretive surroundings. Though she'd seen the large, ornate, well-equipped subterranean chamber beneath the Old Admiralty Building many times, she felt extra tension in the air tonight.

Tonight was undeniably different from many of the others.

She sat at the round table, which was a first; like the great one of the legendary Camelot, traditionally, it was only the knights and the king who ever sat there. Being there with the hard leather frame pressing against her back seemed unnatural, but not because of the material. She was sitting in the shadow of former glories, following in old footsteps.

Experiencing a privilege of the rare few.

Two seats away from her, Kit's expression was uncharacteristically stern. His back was hurting, but he'd experienced worse. He'd replaced his glasses with contacts and taken a paracetamol tablet to temporarily ease his discomfort, knowing that rest would come soon enough.

At the head of the table, two suited men of different yet imposing features had been engaged in conversation with Phil and Jay for well over ten minutes. Though Maria had heard every word, she sensed this was not a conversation for her ears. One of the two she knew well and never questioned. The other she knew less well, yet experience told her that he also deserved similar praise. Both, in their own way, were great and highly respected.

And, tonight, men who were looking for answers.

A knock at the door changed the atmosphere; she was unsure whether it eased the tension or escalated it. Whoever it was, the new arrival was over twenty minutes late and would need to have some good excuses.

Atkins walked towards the door and studied the visitor through the eye slot. The knock had been to a particular beat; Maria associated it with a form of password.

The former head of the MoD opened the door.

Mike entered, his appearance surprisingly presentable. She saw him glance in her direction before sitting between her and Kit, his usual seat at the table. He cleared his throat and sipped slowly from a glass of water, one of twelve laid out.

Mr White stood at the top of the table alongside Atkins, who took a seat. Seeing him at the table was less unusual.

"I'm sure I don't need to remind any of you that anything said here must remain inside these walls. I don't care if the Queen or the PM himself asks you any questions. I trust that is quite clear?"

Heads nodded in unison.

Mr White folded his arms and slowly circled the table. His focus was on Mike. "Hansen. Let's begin with you. I suggest you start at the point where Masterson was beaten up."

Mike took a second sip from his water, ignoring Kit's clear raising of his eyebrows in frustration. He started by going into detail about his leaving the opera house, recalling everything that had happened since: the run, the church, the Tube . . .

"You were at the station and still couldn't catch him?" Kit asked, interrupting.

"Somehow, the bastard's timing was perfect to the second. I was running so fast I couldn't stop myself; only just managed to stay on my feet. Everard was sitting on the other side of the carriage when it left."

"Heading where?" Atkins asked.

"Circle and District eastbound."

"Where does that take him?"

The Bordeaux Connection

"Blackfriars," Maria answered instinctively. "Next up is Mansion House, Cannon Street, Monument and Tower Hill. It also passes Liverpool Street and King's Cross St Pancras."

Atkins bit his lip. "Put out a call to every station on that line. I want all the surveillance footage checked . . ."

"Already taken care of. Footage shows Everard leaving the Tube at Monument and disappearing along Fish Street Hill. I've put out a call for the CCTV footage to be checked from the nearby buildings. That should come in within the next hour."

"You've spoken with the police?" Mr White asked.

"Not directly, but thanks in no small part to the attack on the Royal Opera House being mainstream news, Everard is already the UK's most wanted. Whether people are aware of his identity or not is another matter. The Royal Opera House's own cameras had already confirmed his presence."

"Did it catch him with the Foreign Secretary?" Mike asked.

"I'm still to hear all the details at this stage. However, unfortunately, it did capture him running away from you and Kit."

Mr White cursed under his breath while Atkins slapped his hands on the table.

"Gentlemen," Atkins looked at Mike, Kit and Jay, "I congratulate you. Earlier today, you were given specific orders to keep tabs on the wife of the Deputy Prime Minister. And since that time, you've somehow managed to let this happen under your very noses."

Mike bit his lip, choosing to sip from his water instead of entering arguments. Technically, the evacuation of the Deputy PM and his wife had been a success.

"The bastard was planning on pushing the remote anyway," Kit said, quietly livid. "The size of the blast confirms the attack was intended to spread mass panic."

"Why?" Jay asked. 'If they just wanted the Deputy PM and his missus, why not just target them?"

"Who knows?" Kit replied. "Perhaps they wanted to make the assassination look accidental. After seeing that video late last night, I can't shake the feeling the attack was more on Mrs Hughes than her husband."

"You might have a point," Mr White said, "though a few words from the Foreign Secretary, I'm sure, could help clarify the matter. Speaking of which, where is he now?"

"Upstairs." Kit pointed. "They've put him under temporary house arrest in his apartment. A couple of bobbies were on hand when I arrived at the Cabinet Office."

"At least that's something," Atkins said bluntly. "What news on the death toll?"

"Fifteen for sure," Maria said. "More are in hospital."

"How many?" Kit asked.

"Could be over thirty," Maria replied.

"Good God," Kit said under his breath.

"What news on the substance?" Atkins asked.

"Tests are ongoing," Phil said. "We won't know for sure till samples of the exploded liquid get checked in the lab."

"Where is it now?" Atkins pressed.

"On its way to the lab."

"You weren't interested in finding out yourself?" Mike asked.

"I'd love to, Mikey. However, sadly everyone outside this room still thinks I work for the RAF as a fuel jockey. I did manage to study that photo you sent in more detail."

"And?" Mr White asked.

"Unclear. But based on that one photo alone, coupled with Captain Hansen's eyewitness reports of the colours seen through the X-ray setting of the opera glasses, I'd conclude we could well be dealing with something containing high amounts of nitro-glycerine along with some form of alcohol."

"Nitro . . ." Atkins tailed off. "I thought that stuff went out with the ark."

"It's highly unstable, and most of our contemporaries tend to prefer something more steady. That said, it can still pack a punch if you know what you're doing."

The Bordeaux Connection

Mr White turned to Mike. "What happened after you missed the train?"

"Nothing, really. I got a lecture from some orange jacket who didn't realise who I was."

"What did you tell him?" Kit asked.

"Just the usual guff. That I was undercover and not to ask any stupid questions."

"What happened then?" Maria asked.

"Nothing. I headed for the opposite platform and got a Tube to St James's Park."

"You didn't cause a scene?"

"Not really, assuming you discount the people on the platform thinking I was just some idiot who couldn't use a door."

"Not far wrong," Kit said.

"This isn't a joke – any of you." Atkins turned to Maria. "What news of the DPM's wife?"

"Nothing concrete. Although a woman of her description was seen leaving the Tube at London Bridge. I haven't had a chance to check the footage personally."

"Any word of her husband?"

"Still with the PM. Last I checked, he was trying to make contact."

"Well, he's probably not going to be leaving Number 10 anytime soon, so we can no longer rely on him. What about Mrs Pickering?" Mr White asked.

"Also in the building above. Ironically she's currently being kept in Mr Hughes's apartment. The PM was adamant she be kept away from her husband."

Mr White nodded, his tone subdued. "Well, gentlemen," he looked at Mike, Kit and Jay, "this leaves us with a very unusual situation. Now, as you all know, I've never been one to point the finger. It was a difficult job and you don't need me to lecture you on the consequences of failure. The repercussions of this will no doubt be long lasting. Questions will need to be answered, but right now, they're going to have to wait. I'm sure I don't need to remind any of you what's at stake."

Heads nodded in unison.

"I want every piece of CCTV footage checked. I don't care who you cooperate with," he said, mainly to Maria, "be it the police, the fire department, even the brownies. Any leads we have on Everard could be critical.

"You two." He turned to Mike and Kit. "How are your injuries?"

"Fine," Mike said.

"I suppose I can put off the physio till after my fiancée gets home from work," Kit added.

"What did you say to the Foreign Secretary?" Maria interrupted. "Apparently, he was in a terrible mood when he arrived."

"Well that's hardly surprising, is it? The man had just been arrested."

"Either way, he could still be an important lead for us. Guilty or not, getting in the face of a cabinet minister is rarely a good idea."

"In his defence, I thought he took the news rather calmly."

"He went quietly?" Mike asked.

"It was all fairly routine, if that's what you mean? The bobbies didn't linger on the street either."

"Can I ask a question?" Mike asked. "Why do we not have anyone else working on this?"

"Who says we don't?" Maria replied.

Her response confused him. "There are twelve seats at this table, and only Kit, Jay and me are here. Nine of us are missing."

Mr White looked at him from the far side of the room. "The word absent might be better used in this case, Hansen. Right now, I need you to concentrate on your own job."

Mike nodded. "Yes, sir."

"What happened in that church? You said he gave you some paper?" Maria asked.

"He did – two pieces, in fact. The second exploded in my face, a disguised smoke bomb – I've never seen anything like it so small."

"You have the second?" The question was from Phil.

"Actually, I do, but I haven't dared open it."

"Give it to me." Phil accepted it and walked towards the sink.

"Everard, or whatever the hell his real name is, seemed pretty indifferent to me until I pushed him about his confidence that I was MI5. He then muttered something in French or German, and his attitude changed."

"You revealed your identity?" Kit asked.

"Of course not, but he seemed confident in his own guess. Having spoken to him in the church, I'm guessing we're not exactly unheard of in certain parts of the world."

"Just because we don't officially exist doesn't mean no one's heard of us," Kit said. "I like to think of us as the Illuminati. Or the Elders of Zion."

"Or God?" Jay smiled wryly.

Mr White took a seat in the top chair, its design reminiscent of a throne. "If these people are who we think they are, their knowledge of us will be restricted to folklore. Even if one knew more than he should, it still doesn't change the goalposts. Right now, your conversation with Everard is the only confirmation we have of his involvement – at least besides footage of the actual explosion. Presumably, he didn't talk about Randek?"

"No. Most of the time, he just sneered at me for being young. But, like I say, he seemed to be basing everything on the idea I was MI5."

"How about any background checks?" Kit asked.

"Only what you already know," Phil replied, returning from the sink unscathed. "The man is wanted but lower down the list than most."

"How about the Police? GCHQ? Interpol?"

"No joy, at least not yet. Randek was a different question. It was because of his prominence that alarm bells began to ring in the first place."

"Well, we've already met Everard; we know he's a bastard."

"He revealed nothing of his background?" Atkins asked Mike.

"Not a thing. The man seemed more interested in talking about French history. Huguenots and gallantry."

"Conversations that go nowhere. Intimidation tactics," Maria said.

"So he's actually a woman?" Kit asked.

"You sure there's nothing on Mrs Hughes? If she was the intended target, she could know much," Mike said.

"Last we saw, she was at London Bridge. Probably getting on another train."

"How about her other place? Where is it?"

"Knightsbridge," Jay said. "Been there already."

"You searched it top to bottom?" Kit asked.

"And then some."

"Knightsbridge isn't far from here. Could she have gone back?" Mike asked.

"Unlikely, and trust me, it's covered," Maria said. "There's a reason for the empty seats at this table."

Mike was only slightly reassured. "How about the country residences?"

"A bit of a trek but can't be ruled out." Maria noticed a strange look in Mike's eye. "What are you getting at?"

"I don't like coincidences either, and earlier today, I was reminded of one. Pickering and Hughes share a residence."

"Chevening."

"What trains go from London Bridge?"

"Everywhere. Currently, there are nine platforms. Platform six is notoriously the most crowded in Europe."

"Is it possible she could have headed for Chevening?"

Maria was unsure. "Possibly, but even if you're correct, why return to the scene of the crime?"

"In my experience, that's precisely where most criminals go," Kit said.

"This isn't Arthur Conan Doyle," Maria said, "even if you are something of a hound."

The Bordeaux Connection

"If Mrs Hughes and Pickering were both involved with Randek, at least up to a point, it stands to reason Chevening could have been the hub. Has it been checked?"

"Not yet, but under the circumstances, such things cannot be ignored." Mr White nodded, his dynamic eyes focused on Mike and Kit. "I want both of you to get right on it. A car will be waiting for you outside the citadel in two minutes. If she is currently seated aboard a train to Kent, you've every chance of beating her to it. If you do find her, I don't want her to leave the building unescorted."

Mike nodded.

Kit asked, "And if she isn't there?"

"There's nothing else we can do until Everard reappears on the radar. So either way, I don't want you out of Kent before morning."

The car was already there when they left the building. Mike took the wheel while Jay rode shotgun. Kit lay with his feet up in the back, complaining of his injury.

The orders were to drop Jay off in Knightsbridge. His reconnaissance of the apartment earlier that day had come up with nothing. Now, however, the plan was different.

"If Hughes's wife did return to Knightsbridge, it's possible she's already left," Mike said, driving west. Though it was after 9 p.m., the traffic was still heavy around Westminster and The Mall. "Not that you'll be hoping she's there."

Kit was unconvinced. "If she's gone to Knightsbridge, why the hell did she get the Tube to London Bridge?"

"A panic move. Convenience. Throw us off the scent, maybe?"

"Putting her expenses to good use." Jay smiled.

"Well, just be careful," Kit warned. "Judging by her form earlier today, if she catches you in the act, she'll probably throw you off the building."

Jay grinned back via the mirror. "I'll bear it in mind."

Mike smiled, catching Jay from the side. Someone of Asian origin working in the White Hart would have been a no-no just fifteen years ago, but the boy had made history. He'd never met a man so positive about life.

Mike took a left turn, following the satnav. "According to this, we're looking at no more than ten minutes." He restrained his impulse to add, "Assuming the traffic remains as it is." His thoughts had already turned to Chevening. "Where the hell is this estate?"

"Heart of Kent, near Tonbridge." Kit sat up in the back seat. After lying on his back, moving felt strange. "Not the kind of place one usually arrives at unannounced in the middle of the night."

"You talking from experience?" Jay asked.

"No. But let's just say I know the type, and I'd hate to be on the receiving end after a bad day at the office."

Mike nodded, his eyes on the road. The traffic was flowing, which was good; their chances of beating the train were poor. The last thing they needed was to hit delays.

As they headed away from Westminster, the fine buildings of history replaced by those of wealth and status, his mind recalled his conversation with Everard in the church. The White Hart were a strange band; despite five years as a Red Beret, he'd never heard of them before the day he signed up. It was an invitation few received, one he would never have received again should he have said no early on. When he said yes, there was no going back. How a Frenchman could have heard of them was difficult to know.

But a question that he guessed would be answered sooner or later.

In the secret room below the Old Admiralty Building, Mr White scrutinised the screen of his mobile phone. He felt sure that a call from the Prime Minister was likely before sunrise. In past years, he'd not been unaccustomed to receiving one on his personal number. However, these days it seemed an unnecessary risk. Even if the conversation wasn't overheard from abroad, the last thing he needed was GCHQ knowing his every thought.

Maria was still seated in the same place, tapping on a laptop. "Confirmation from London Bridge. Mrs Hughes was seen boarding a train that terminates in Tonbridge."

Mr White nodded. Although it was possible she could have taken it elsewhere, as the route would take her within twelve miles of her husband's country estate, it seemed likely that was her destination.

"Let Hansen and Masterson know. This could be of direct relevance."

"Yes, sir."

Phil was standing in the corner of the room where two years earlier, he'd constructed a makeshift laboratory. The two pieces of paper Mike had received from Everard were folded up near the sink.

Mr White walked in his direction. "Any update on the . . . well, you know?"

Phil passed him the first piece. "Classic smoke bomb. Small, but effective."

Mr White took the remains of the paper in his hand. He saw burn marks around the outside and evidence of some sort of grey powder. "Have you ever seen anything of the type before?"

"Similar, but not identical. I'd say it comes in bigger sizes."

Mr White returned him the scattered remains. "And the other thing?"

"Well, it's not a weapon . . . I suggest you see for yourself."

He unfolded the paper and gave it to Mr White. A single page folded into eight was partially crumpled from being in Mike's pocket.

The Director looked at it for several seconds. There was handwriting, words written in French. At first, he struggled to believe his eyes. Then as the seconds passed, realisation dawned.

"Good God!"

Kent
23:00

It was dark beyond the hills. Darker still on the roads. The streets were deserted and had been for some time. Even in the main towns, the area wasn't the most populated of places. The largest had about 60,000 residents, but there were days when it could appear to be much less. The work was usually related to the high street, much of which had been affected by modern times. The Internet age was a wonderful thing unless you were a high-street retailer. As prices fell, shoppers celebrated. That was the theory. It had held true in every walk of life since the Stone Age. Everyone loves value for money.

Unless you're a seller.

The villages that dotted the landscape had long been sources of legend. Like the picturesque dwellings of Cornwall and Ireland or the legendary valleys of Wales, there was something about the Kent countryside that cried out mystery. Most of the villages were said to be haunted, be it by lost-in-time Romans, cursed Vikings or little girls who failed to do as their father told them; each one had a story to tell. Even some of the modern inhabitants were inclined to believe them, especially those who grew up with the tales. Those who didn't believe them often played a part in creating them.

It was an alternative way a business could thrive without the high street.

Within the county's famous rolling countryside, whose sights had inspired artists, writers and poets throughout the ages, the North Downs were difficult to miss. Unlike the nearby world-renowned towns and cities, there were no international railway stations or evidence of mass transport infrastructure to scar the landscape. The scenery, instead, was more at one with bygone times. Chalk hills were rare in England but a prominent feature in the south-east. What began in Surrey as an iconic hill line was also a significant feature of the countryside all the way to the sea. It had been claimed that the scenery on the coast was even more special: an area that, in its own way, had helped win England a war – perhaps many. Even before the days of Vera Lynn, there was something about the white chalk cliffs that could lift the spirits of even the most down-heartened onlooker. The conservationists designated it an Area of Outstanding Natural Beauty. Those who knew them best needed only one of those words:

Outstanding.

Among the isolated residential areas on the North Downs, the village of Chevening was easy to miss. Like the surrounding hills, visually, it was a throwback to a slower time when the sound of metal on metal was more likely than an explosion in an opera house. The parish was smaller than most. The latest census indicated the population was less than 3,000, with many more coming as tourists. Most visitors came for the walks; even in the modern day, the Pilgrims' Way, once famed in Middle England as the route to Becket's Shrine, still swept through the landscape. According to local historians, it wasn't just pilgrims who had walked the pathways. The Home Guard had famously kept a watchful vigil against the Nazis. A thousand years earlier, a different group of Englishmen had even more famously done the same, their way to Hastings lit by a comet. It was once said that whoever controlled the area controlled England.

Little had changed in a thousand years.

The house itself was newer than many in the village. According to its historical records, the fine Grade I listed Jacobean mansion that governed the 3,500-acre estate had been built on the site of something much older. Its legacy belonged entirely to one family. Reading up on the facts, Mike couldn't help but sense a ring of familiarity about it. What began with soldiers ended with statesmen. As the decades rolled by, the focus changed: war craft to extravagant architecture. As always, it ended with art. Mike had been inside enough government buildings to know a number housed valuable collections. If the size of Chevening was anything to go by, it would probably be the mother and father of them.

A legacy created by earls and extended by politicians.

The journey had taken just under an hour, even abiding by the speed limit. Following the directions of the BMW's inbuilt satnav system, a ten-mile stretch along the A2 was completed in less than ten minutes. Joining the M25 at junction 2, the journey continued steadily. At this hour, the traffic was light, and there were no speed restrictions to contend with; even if there had been, Mike knew Kit would have been in two minds about sticking to them. A quiet word in the right ear would usually take care of these matters, but, in other ways, it was one of the greatest conundrums of the job. Speed usually meant greater efficiency, but doing a job where livelihood depended on anonymity, it could also create difficulties. The flashing blue lights and deafening sirens of authority could be a magnet for unwanted interest.

Fortunately, the BMW was unlikely to attract such notice.

Mike took the turn off the motorway, following which a series of roads and roundabouts took them deep into the countryside. It felt like being in the heart of England – green fields, woodlands, quiet country roads that could lead anywhere. If the satnav was correct, they were less than two miles away.

"Eyes peeled," Kit said, scanning the countryside. "Even cabinet ministers aren't stupid enough to give away their exact address."

Mike nodded, guessing he had a point. The signs suggested they were on Chevening Road, a clue Mike thought, if nothing else. Following the road, the signs confirmed they'd entered an area called Chipstead, a village that could have been a hamlet. As the long, narrow road continued north, several houses appeared on both sides, their façades an attractive mixture of modern and red brick Victorian. There were cars parked on the road, compensating for the lack of driveways, but they were still to find anything with lights on.

The Bordeaux Connection

Further on, the countryside returned, the occasional mansion surrounded by tall trees and hedging. Across the motorway, the houses disappeared, replaced by mile upon mile of greenery that seemingly headed forever into the distance. They were getting close, Mike thought again – only a government building could exist in such seclusion, yet also so strangely close to London. Up ahead, he saw houses, a church tower rising above them in the distance. A long wall on the left caught his attention; the land beyond it was veiled by bricks and large trees. In contrast to the wholly accessible open space across the road, everything about the location cried out privacy.

Unquestionably, they had made it.

Visually, the village matched his expectations. The redbrick frontages of the cottages were laden in ivy, a postcard image of a forgotten time. Again, there were cars parked on both sides of the road, but nothing was moving. The occasional light coming from one of the cottage windows was the exception rather than the norm.

"Eyes peeled, Michael," he heard Kit say again, not that it was necessary. According to the satnav, less than half a mile remained.

Up ahead, several signs came into view. One caught Mike's eye: *Private Road*, preceding a large wooden gate situated between two red walls of varying height. The walls were of similar construction, though more clearly visible than the one he had passed a short distance back. He braked, coming to a standstill, and looked at Kit.

"Shall we drive all the way? Or continue by foot?"

Kit's preference would have been to enter the grounds the old-fashioned way. Stealth, lightless, unnoticed. The lack of light was their best asset – that and the trees. The estate contained over 3,000 acres, but he could tell from the GPS they were a lot closer than that to the main house. A quick hop over the wall and they would come to a small area of woodland, dense enough to cover their approach. All that would remain would be to gain entry.

Tonight, he knew, the actual plan would be different. Unlike the clandestine affair of earlier in the day, the Deputy Prime Minister had officially agreed to their visit.

Mike drove to the main gate, where he was met by a security guard in uniform who saluted half-heartedly as Mike passed over his ID.

"Good evening. I believe we're expected."

The security guard examined his card under the torchlight. "Follow the road to the left, Captain. You can park outside the house."

"Thank you."

The estate office was located on the right. Like at Chequers and Dorneywood, the house was officially owned and managed by a separate trust and allocated to the Prime Minister per the late owner's will. There were lights on in the estate buildings, unlike the house itself.

The house was a picture; neither of them had expected anything less. Even at night, the three-storey red brick building was like something out of a fairy tale. A well-maintained stone flight of steps led up to three rounded archways that provided the base for four Doric columns that supported a triangular gable above the third storey. Standing adjacent to the main building, two sister buildings faced one another, connected by curved walls lined with hedging. Like the house itself, everything about the layout was perfectly symmetrical. Completing the design, a circular lawn occupied the space between the three buildings, the grass recently cut and smelling of spring. At the centre was a stone ornament; using the night-vision setting on his opera glasses, Mike saw it was a birdbath.

They left the car and approached the entrance, Mike armed with a set of keys. Inserting the correct one, he felt a sense of anti-climax.

"Hang about. You never know. There may be staff inside who don't know we're coming."

160

Kit began to laugh. "Staff? Where do you think this is – Windsor?"

Mike turned the key, eyeing Kit with the usual scepticism of not knowing whether he was joking. The door creaked as it opened, revealing a grand hallway with a white tiled floor and a spiral staircase that led to the floor above.

The entire house seemed deserted.

"The quickest a train can arrive from London Bridge to Sevenoaks is twenty-eight minutes," Mike said, recalling the data on the BMW's command console. "If she's coming, she should be here by now."

"Apparently, she was going to Tonbridge. Of course, then she would have to wait for a cab." A thought entered Kit's mind. "Maria, are you there?"

Maria had left the Old Admiralty Building. She was now sitting behind the wheel of a car parked close to Knightsbridge.

"Loud and clear. What's your position?"

Kit replied, "Inside. No sign of life. Not even from the staff." He glanced at Mike.

"Good work. What's it look like in there?"

"Well, it's suitable for a lady. Perhaps even a duchess," he said, quietly aware that Prince Charles had once turned the place down. Further along, he saw a series of long corridors with oak bookcases lined with red carpet. "What's the earliest she could have arrived?"

"The train was for Tonbridge. Current reports say it arrived forty minutes ago. Assuming she was still on it, she should be with you pretty soon."

"I thought she was definitely on it?"

"Unfortunately, Sevenoaks and Tonbridge are less equipped with CCTV, so we can't entirely rule out the possibility that she got off at an earlier station."

He decided to let her off the hook. "What are we looking for?"

"If a link does exist between Mrs Hughes and Pickering, there may be evidence of something somewhere. There's a study on the first floor. Apparently, it's close to the living quarters. See what you can find."

"Roger that!"

Mike had already climbed the stairs, deciding not to wait for Kit. He saw light coming from somewhere. For now, he was unsure whether it was from inside the house.

The landing was carpeted, the walls a subtle shade of red that matched the exterior. Portraits and masterpieces from the estate's heyday lined the route, the majority relating to war or hunting. The doorways were symmetrical, most of them partially open. Mike searched each room as he passed, espying opulent furnishings ready for use.

He heard a noise in his ear. "Grosmont, give me your position."

"First floor, third room on the left. Proceeding to the one opposite."

"What's it look like up there?"

"How about you come see for yourself?"

"Maybe in a few minutes. First, I want to finish with the downstairs."

"Roger that."

The main hall was abundant in wood and rich upholstery. The walls were oak panelled that matched the bannisters on the main stairs.

The living area was in keeping with his initial assumptions and had clearly been lived in recently. There was fruit in a bowl on a coffee table, along with several magazines of various genres. Ignoring the temptation to take a look, Kit passed the rooms quickly and headed for the other side of the house.

There were no signs of life; had it not been for his prior knowledge, he'd probably have dismissed the house as something of little significance. Through the windows on the far side, he studied the grounds. There was a lake in the distance; moonlight cast an ethereal glow on the water. With the lack of light coming from inside the house, it seemed brighter than usual, reminding him he was alone.

"How's it going up there?"

Mike replied, "Thirty rooms in. All much the same."

"Any open drawers? Half-packed suitcases? Rent boys locked away in cupboards?"

Mike laughed. "Nothing so far, though I'll keep checking. Place feels more like a museum."

"Yes, it does, doesn't it? Keep in close contact. We don't want any ghoulies to surprise us when we're taking a leak."

He returned to the area where he saw the bookcases. They reminded him of the footage from the night before: the Raleigh manuscript now in the hands of a wanted terrorist. In his mind, he considered the report from Edinburgh. Several missing items, mostly art and manuscripts.

He guessed there was a connection.

"Grosmont, you love your history. Who were the family who lived here before?"

"Earls of Stanhope."

"Who were they?"

"Landowners and distant cousins of the royals."

"Anyone important?"

"I think there might have been a connection with Mountbatten."

"Understood. Why steal something by Walter Raleigh?"

Entering another bedroom on the first floor, Mike paused. "Come again?"

"It never really clicked into place last night. Perhaps it was fatigue. The Raleigh manuscript. Who would steal something like that?"

Mike was unsure. "Collectors. Drug traffickers. Arms dealers . . ."

"Why drug traffickers and arms dealers?"

"Collateral, usually. They only have limited resale value compared to what they're worth when legal. If a gang needs collateral for a loan, it's usually a popular choice."

"You think it was stolen for that? And the stuff from Edinburgh?"

In truth, Mike still had no idea. "Well, I'm not gonna lie to you, Kit. I can think of better things. The only other reason must be so specific I can't even think of it yet."

"You know, I was afraid you might say something like that."

Mike left the room and crossed the corridor, entering the room opposite. Instead of a lavish bedroom, a king-sized bed lined with linen sheets, this one appeared to be used as a study. He explored it in detail, following a red carpet intercepted by several lines of bookcases. There were so many it reminded him of a library. Another door in the far wall led through to an area furnished with a large oak desk flanked by filing cabinets.

"Hey, come upstairs when you can. I think I've just found something."

"What?"

"A library. I'm guessing this was what Maria meant by study."

"Roger that. I'll be right up."

Mike moved on. He explored the bookcases in the half-light and stopped by one row in particular. He recognised names: editions of every work of fiction from Jane Austen to Laurence Sterne; he guessed many had never been opened.

There was light entering from a nearby window. The views were far reaching, including the lake, the woodland and a walled garden south-west of the house. Close to the walled garden, he saw a car on the driveway, a small red thing, possibly a Corsa. He considered speaking to Kit but decided against it, again guided by instinct.

The door to the second room was still open; a computer was on the desk, presently in sleep mode. Mike entered and activated the screen, annoyed that it was password protected. Removing Phil's portable hacking device from his belt, he inserted it into the USB port and began digging through the filing cabinets.

No luck! He could tell instantly he was looking at things connected to the Trust. He checked them all and returned to the screen. The device had worked.

"Edward, what was the password for Hughes's office?"

"Lavinia. Why?"

"I've just come up with one that was Valerie."

"Where are you?"

"Fifteenth door on your right, through the library. Sitting at a computer."

Mike clicked on the mouse and started to explore the desktop. Though the machine had been in sleep mode, he judged from the evidence it had been used recently. The web browser was up, including one for Yahoo.

Whoever had used it, he guessed it wasn't the Foreign Secretary.

He heard footsteps in the corridor; from his seat, it wasn't obvious whether they were heading in his direction.

"Edward, come in here. Come check this out."

The footsteps had stopped, then started again. They appeared louder. Apparently running.

Mike jumped to his feet and left the room, heading through the library.

"Edward? Edward?" There was a light on somewhere along the corridor, a distant glow coming from inside one of the rooms. He moved quickly, keeping close to the walls. Removing his gun, he stopped outside the door, peered inside and entered.

He froze, his arms outstretched. Kit was standing by the bed holding a gun.

Aimed at the wife of the Deputy PM.

Admiralty House, Whitehall
23:15

Standing guard outside the door of one of the three special apartments within Admiralty House, the duty policeman saluted the smartly dressed gentleman marching in his direction. Though he didn't recognise him personally, there was something about the man's gait and appearance that cried out top brass.

"Good evening, sir."

"Good evening," the visitor replied, showing him an ID badge. Sure enough, the man was armed forces. RAF retired.

"I'm here to have a chat with the Foreign Secretary."

The Foreign Secretary was lying on the couch, watching a film downloaded from on demand. The news channels were all concerned with one subject, and – *thanks to the impertinent fellow with the dark-rimmed glasses* – he wasn't going to be leaving before dawn.

He heard a key turn in the lock, followed by the opening of the front door. A man entered, instantly recognisable.

"Good God. I might have known."

Mr White approached the couch and sat down in an armchair directly opposite him. He eased the seat within inches of the nearby coffee table and looked the Foreign Secretary in the eye.

"Now then, Richard. What say the two of us have a little chat? Just you and me. Won't that be nice?"

From a payphone in the main concourse of Dover Priory train station, a call was currently being placed to a number in Paris.

The caller wasn't used to being clean-shaven. He'd bought himself a razor from a retailer at St Pancras and hogged the toilet on the first available train. After ten years without a shave, the phone's plastic casing gave off a tingling sensation against his skin.

The dialling tone bleeped in his ear: four, five, six . . . *where the hell is Randek?*

An answer. "*Allô?*"

"It is I."

The man in Paris sat upright in his chair. "They have been talking about your exploits for hours. Even in France, you are being heralded as a maniac or a hero." He gripped the phone tightly as he rose to his feet, his eyes on the street outside his office window, his view partially restricted by the closed blinds. "They say on the news over fifteen have been killed. They also say no one of status."

"Plans are subject to change."

"What happened?"

"If you watch the news, you have already heard what happened. The Security Service are not fools. They watch as we do. Some more closely than others."

Unbeknownst to Everard, the man in Paris nodded in understanding. "You are safe?"

"Safer than I was two hours ago."

"Is your line secure? Can you talk? Where are you now?"

The cellist decided an answer, albeit from a payphone with no evidence connecting him with the location, would be a mistake. "*En route.* The Eurostar finishes at eight; I had to make other arrangements."

At the other end, the man from Paris nodded again. He was calling from the ferry port or the airport, he mused.

"When you return, I might have a little present for you." Randek edged towards his desk and picked up an item of jewellery. "It seems my sister is most fond of you. Perhaps I have been harsh on you all these years."

"You honestly think this is the time." Everard took a long breath. "We can talk when I return. What are my instructions?"

167

"Return safe and return unnoticed – your instructions are no different than before. When you are back in France, there will be people who want to meet with you."

"Are they from Paris? Marseille?"

"Neither. However, head to Paris. That will put you on the right track – after that, we can head south together. Be careful of the transport police. You never know. They might suspect you of being an asylum seeker." He laughed loudly.

Everard replaced the phone and rubbed his clean-shaven face as he headed for the main exit. The journey to the ferry port would take less than ten minutes by taxi.

Giving him less than twenty to get aboard the ferry.

Alone in the quiet office, Randek cleared the line without replacing the receiver and put through a second call. The occurrences of the previous three days had already made a mark on the continent. Security had been heightened; inquests would be imminent, repercussions inevitable. Success in two ventures was now assured.

All that remained was the final one.

Chevening
23:35

Mike leaned closer to the woman on the couch and flicked the wheel on the cigarette lighter. He held his hand steady as the tip of her cigarette caught the flame, her eyes focusing mesmerisingly on his as she exhaled.

The last ten minutes had been among the longest of Mike's life. The woman was a bag of nerves, worse now than she'd been on fleeing the opera house. Her appearance had changed since then. Her face carried less make-up, particularly around her eyes and cheeks, as though she'd made an improvised attempt to disguise her appearance.

Mike was exhausted. Being in the White Hart was never an easy job. Yet there was something about dealing with heartbroken women that was even worse than dealing with the villains. A career in active service had taught him to adapt to new scenarios, but he knew no training could have prepared him for the last few days. His grandfather had once told him about his experiences at Arnhem in the war. What began as a mission that went seriously wrong ended in a cat-and-mouse chase to evade the Nazis. He'd escaped along the river in a small dinghy before heading across country back towards Allied lines, eventually being picked up by the Americans.

He'd barely slept in ninety-six hours.

Mike lowered his hand and backed away from the politician's wife, taking a seat on the couch. He thought about asking her a question but decided against it, concluding that she needed time to gather herself.

Kit took a seat adjacent to Mike, an antique armchair that had clearly been passed through the generations. He removed his mobile phone from his pocket and began navigating the desktop.

He stopped on reaching a folder in the picture gallery where he had earlier received a data transfer from Charlestown.

Kit smiled sympathetically. "Do you have any idea who we are?"

Mrs Hughes inhaled her cigarette and flicked ash into an ashtray on the nearest table, another antique feature decorated with the emblem of the former owners.

"Does it matter?"

Mike raised an eyebrow; Kit replied, "Not to us."

She blew smoke, her eyes taking in their features. "You must be MI5. No one else predicts a terrorist attack seconds before it goes off then turns up unannounced in the country estate of the man who was the intended target." She looked them both in the eye in turn. "How did you know?"

"It's our job," Mike said, again satisfied by the incorrect assumption that they worked for MI5.

"Why are you here?"

Kit handed over his mobile phone, showing her the photos. "I assume this needs no clarification?"

The photo was clear-cut. King's Cross, dusk, platform three. She was standing alongside a man of French features, carrying what appeared to be a historical manuscript.

Colour drained from her face. "How did you know?"

"We know a lot of things." Kit avoided the temptation to repeat, 'it's our job'. "You know that man?"

"Not really."

"Then why were you meeting him?"

She shrugged.

"Less than twenty-four hours earlier, you were caught on CCTV removing a historical manuscript named *The Ocean to Cynthia* by Walter Raleigh from the library at Montacute House. Why?" The question came from Mike.

She puffed again at her cigarette and blew smoke towards the ceiling. The hostility of her expression concerned him. He remembered an analogy his grandfather had once given him.

The Bordeaux Connection

A wounded animal is most deadly when it's cornered.

Kit scrolled through the photographs and stopped on seeing one of Everard talking with the Foreign Secretary.

"You recognise this man?"

She delayed, concentrating on her cigarette, clearly afraid of what she might see.

Her face relaxed slightly. "That's the Foreign Secretary."

Obviously. "Do you recognise the man with him?"

She took the phone and studied it for several seconds. Finally, she shook her head.

"This photo was taken earlier tonight close to the lobby of the Royal Opera House," Kit began. "It was taken at 19:46, exactly twelve minutes before the bomb went off, exactly seven minutes before my associate evacuated you and your husband from Box 63. It was this man who set off the explosion."

Mrs Hughes exhaled nervously and tipped away further ash. Kit expected her to speak, but she didn't.

Again, Mike was pleased she was still holding everything together.

"I take it you've never seen him before?" Kit asked. "He wasn't known to you?"

"No." She seemed baffled by the question. "Why? Should he be?"

"Well, he's certainly well known to your housemate. Seems a little odd, don't you think? The Foreign Secretary chatting with a man who intended to kill you."

She wiped tears from her eyes but didn't answer.

"The man in the picture we understand to be well known to the man you met at King's Cross," Mike said, his tone softer than Kit's. "We even have reports that the man has a son with *Monsieur* Randek's sister. What's your relationship with Randek?"

This time she answered. "I only met him once."

"At the station?"

"Yes."

"What does your husband think of all this?"

She delayed giving an answer. "He doesn't know."

"Why did you steal the book from Montacute House?" Mike repeated. A gut feeling told him there was a connection between the articles taken from Edinburgh and the Raleigh book. "Who put you up to it?"

Fresh tears fell from her eyes. "It was Richard. He was responsible for everything."

"He blackmailed you into stealing the book?" Kit asked.

"Yes."

"Why?" Mike asked.

She shook her head. "He never said."

"What did he say?"

"He told me he needed me to do him a favour."

"You decided to accept?"

"I had no choice."

"Over what?"

"He said if I didn't do it, he'd tell my husband."

"Tell him what?" The question came from Kit.

Tears streamed down her face. "Tell him what happened between us."

Mike and Kit exchanged glances. Though Kit said no words, Mike knew exactly what he was thinking.

I definitely prefer the villains.

In the half-light of a deserted room somewhere in France, the dark-haired listener heard something that stood out among the numerous background noises.

Two men were engaged in animated discussion. Though he didn't recognise their voices, the information he was getting from the data software confirmed that both matched those on file. One of them had been set to amber, meaning he was a medium-high priority. The other was purple, a rare colour.

Its exact meaning was restricted to above his pay level.

He typed quickly on his keyboard, making a note of everything that was said. The phone numbers used, though not attributed to any specific people or property, were listed as non-core. In his experience, the non-cores were often the ones the villains would never think had been tapped.

As the conversation ended, he dialled a three-digit extension and waited for an answer.

"*Allô?*"

He recognised the voice of his superior and told him everything he'd witnessed.

"Stay where you are. I shall be right with you."

Maria saw Jay approach from the bottom of the street. No sooner had he entered the car than she shifted into first gear and accelerated away, circling Hyde Park.

"I've just received word from Mike. The DPM's wife has turned up at Chevening."

"Might help explain why I didn't see her here." He smiled.

"Any signs of entry?"

"Negative. The apartment hasn't changed since this morning."

She figured as much. "How about the rest of the place?"

"Nothing new."

"You sure you checked everything?"

Jay stared back, playful yet unimpressed. "You're perfectly welcome to try."

Maria smiled and concentrated on the road, waiting for the traffic to clear before heading back towards Whitehall. Her assumptions were once again bearing out. The key to unlocking the mystery would be to target the Foreign Secretary himself. And that left two possible options.

One of which Mike and Kit were dealing with right now.

Chevening
23:48

Mike and Kit stood in the grand hallway, leaving Mrs Hughes alone in the lounge. Mike watched her from the doorway as she cried into a handkerchief.

He brushed his thumb and index finger across his eyebrows. "Pickering and Hughes." He shook his head, trying to remove the recently conceived image from his mind. "Who would have thought it?"

Kit was busy examining his phone. "Oh, I don't know. Wife of a colleague; sharing the same estate."

"You think the four of them stayed here together?"

"Perhaps. I'm sure if we asked a few subtle questions, it would be easy enough to find out." He looked conspicuously through the doorway into the lounge before guiding Mike out of sight. "Between you and me, I know a few journalists who would pay pretty big for this."

Mike laughed. "I reckon I could find a few myself."

They returned to the lounge five minutes later, carrying freshly made coffee and a plate of biscuits. Kit had made a joke to Mike in the corridor about expenses.

Mike sat down in the same seat. He sipped his coffee for the first time, taking a second to savour the long-awaited caffeine rush.

"I understand your husband and the Foreign Secretary have been sharing the house since Mr Pickering's promotion. How does that work exactly?"

Mrs Hughes seemed confused by the question. "How does what work?"

The Bordeaux Connection

"Well, are you often here together? Do you draw up a rota? One weekend on, one weekend off."

She replaced her mug on the table, ensuring it rested on a coaster. "I assume the real question you want to know is, how did we get away with it?"

Kit raised an eyebrow. Though technically it wasn't part of their job, he was still curious. "I suppose the PM might have hoped a house this size would have been large enough to keep both of his key allies happy."

The woman was unimpressed. "It only happened once. Recently. Usually, only one of us is present at one time."

"So you do use rotas?" Mike asked.

"No. My husband is a busy man, the Foreign Secretary perhaps busier still. As with his predecessor, together, we all came to an understanding. Should all of us want to use the house at the same time, the estate would be more than capable of accommodating us. So far, it's only happened on three occasions."

"But you said it was recent?" Mike asked.

"Three weeks ago, the PM asked my husband to help entertain some important visitors from France. Diplomats of some sort . . . I've never really been much interested in affairs of state."

Mike hid a smile.

"As our visitors were foreign, and as the Foreign Secretary had no other pressing engagement that weekend, it was only natural he would also attend. The evening began with canapés – delicious they were, too. We dined at around eight, and shortly afterwards, my husband went to bed. Christopher's never really been much of a drinker."

The information matched the reports. "So it was just the three of you?"

"Six of us. The diplomats enjoyed their wine. Their wives were not with us. After Rachel went to bed, it was just the four of them and me."

A thousand thoughts were going through Mike's mind. He knew he dared not even consider what was going through Kit's.

"As the evening wore on, I excused myself. By 1 a.m., our visitors had gone to bed. I was in the kitchen cleaning up. That was when Richard walked in."

"I think we get the picture," Mike said.

Kit was annoyed. "Then what happened?"

"Clearly, I'd had too much to drink. The next day I woke up remembering very little." Her hands trembled as she sipped her coffee. "Later that day, Christopher took two of the boys across the estate. Rachel was out shopping. It was just myself, Richard and one of the visitors."

"Randek?" Mike guessed.

"No. I never knew his name. Richard threatened me over what happened. He said he'd tell my husband unless I did them a favour."

"Steal the book?"

She nodded, clearly ashamed.

"Why go ahead? If it came to it, why not deny the affair and tell your husband you were being manipulated?"

Kit shook his head, and the woman laughed without humour. "This is Westminster, darling. And believe me, Richard Pickering is not a man to be taken lightly."

Mike frowned. It still seemed an extreme request for a one-night stand. "I take it no one else knows."

"You two know."

"Well, you needn't worry about us. We're required by law to keep restricted information confidential."

"Ha! You MI5 boys love your code of secrecy, don't you? You know, I've always thought it was an Oxbridge thing. Honour among class. Honour among thieves," she scoffed.

"Fortunately, Mike here went to Loughborough," Kit interjected.

Mike pressed on. "What happened tonight?"

The woman laughed again. "It sounds to me as if you already know."

"Whose idea was it – Dvořák?"

The Bordeaux Connection

"Richard's."

Mike could tell from her face she was furious. "You agreed to attend?"

"Christopher was delighted. Then again, he's never been slow to show goodwill to a colleague," she huffed. "Always been a fan, you know? Opera. Musicals. Even ballet. He's been a patron for over ten years."

"You're certain your husband didn't know?"

"Well, I certainly didn't tell him if that's what you mean?"

"Earlier tonight, you narrowly avoided being killed. At least a dozen people were not so lucky. Whoever's behind it clearly didn't do it simply to do away with you; it's all much too elaborate. All you needed to do was keep quiet. What happened tonight was a risk: one that's backfired."

She shook her head. "I suppose you'll have to ask my husband's housemate."

At precisely 23:50, the Director of the White Hart exited the private apartment in Admiralty House.

The same constable was waiting by the door.

"Keep an eye on this one, won't you? I'm afraid he's just had a bit of a shock."

Mrs Hughes was sitting by one of the kitchen windows, taking in the view. Once upon a time, she'd adored the sight of moonlight reflecting off the lake, but tonight it seemed grim and remote as if she was looking at a barren wilderness.

"So what happens to me now?"

Mike was sitting on a barstool in the kitchen, a modern item that he guessed had been added by one of the present tenants.

"Well, that depends. CCTV at Montacute House caught you stealing a valuable manuscript. The next day, you were photographed giving the same item to a man at King's Cross who just so happens to be wanted in connection with events in Edinburgh."

She looked at him. Though she was no longer crying, her face appeared drawn. "Depends on what? You're not telling me I'm actually being considered a suspect?"

Mike left his seat on the barstool and moved to a sun lounger close to the window. He slid it closer to the politician's wife, her eyes watching his every move.

"At least a dozen people have been killed tonight. At least fifty have been injured over the past three days. Even before tonight, your husband and the PM had a major crisis on their hands; now they're dealing with something a hundred times greater. Now, you may not have been directly involved in tonight's events. But you have been photographed having direct contact with someone who has a connection to at least one of the attacks. Even if you're not a direct suspect, you've found yourself a link in the chain."

"For what?" She made a spitting gesture. "A drunken night of pleasure. And I use that word loosely. The history of Westminster is a sordid tale; even Major was a victim of that. I used to think there was something in the water. Now I know: it was the vodka."

A half smile. "What was the manuscript?"

She lit a cigarette and blew smoke. "A book of poetry."

"Can you elaborate?"

"Literature never was my strong point."

"Why did they want it?"

She looked at him, her eyes piercing with aggression. "I don't know, I didn't ask."

Mike moved slightly nearer and smiled softly. "The Security Service has been watching you for three days. We know you took a Tube to London Bridge. We also know you caught a train to Tonbridge. We knew you were coming here. Fail to cooperate, and it's only a matter of time before the bigwigs queue up to start questioning you. It only takes one leak, a tweet from a worried onlooker, a video on YouTube, and you're looking at a media hell storm."

She laughed humourlessly. "Are you blackmailing me? Or perhaps offering me a deal to save my reputation?"

The Bordeaux Connection

"If this gets out, it's the end of your husband's career. Not to mention all the damage it'll do to the present government. The Foreign Secretary is already looking at a bottomless pit. The PM is going to need the rest of his Cabinet to stay together."

"You care about politics?"

"No. But I care about the safety of our citizens. The media was already prophesying the next al-Qaeda attack before Edinburgh; now we're just a misdirected nuke away from a Fourth Reich. The best thing that can happen is for the man responsible for tonight and the man you met at King's Cross to be captured. At least that will break the chain."

"What do you expect me to do about it?"

Mike looked her straight in the eye. "For starters, how about you tell me in plain and simple terms everything you know."

Kit was upstairs on the landing, talking on the phone. Mike appeared at the top of the stairs just as he was hanging up.

"Sharon," he said, slightly awkwardly. "She does worry."

Mike decided to let it go. "I was just having a chat with the DPM's wife." He laughed spontaneously. "She certainly knows a few stories about Westminster."

Kit placed his phone in his pocket. "They didn't involve any Chelsea kits, did they?"

Mike grinned. "Not exactly. Though apparently, Mr Pickering has long had something of a colourful reputation among the benches. Between you and me, I genuinely can't decide if we're talking Don Juan or David Blunkett."

"Well, his wife seemed complicit enough to have been party to recent proceedings. Better yet, the jackass clearly likes her enough not to wish her dead, which is more than can be said for poor Mrs Hughes. What about these diplomats?"

"Interesting. She gave me some names – not that she needed to. It was an official visit attended by at least a dozen staff; the PM met them the next day. Apparently, it was in aid of something called the Chevening Scholarship."

"I've heard of that. One of my cousins was most put out to have missed out on it. Anyway, what about it?"

"While the PM's appearance was rare and unexpected, the timing seems coincidental. However, it does confirm that there were plenty of people to have witnessed their attendance – including, perhaps, the PM. Maybe Maria can find what we need."

"You think the diplomats were involved?"

"Seems at least one of them was party to the blackmail. They were from the correct country, though apparently Bordeaux as opposed to Marseille."

"That's not the first time the city's been mentioned."

"Exactly. At the end of the day, would you take the risk?"

"Fair point. How's she now?"

"Gone to bed with a G&T and a cigarette. Thief or not, I can't help feeling sorry for her."

"Come along now, Michael. Duty first."

"Be that as it may, would you be okay if your housemate tried to blow you up after sleeping with him?"

Kit gave Mike a weird look. "Well, I suppose I'd try to apologise for my drunken behaviour first."

Mike smiled. "Anyway, I tried asking her questions about Everard and Randek. I thought she might let a few secrets slip once she'd calmed down."

"And?"

"She still claims to have known nothing about Edinburgh or tonight. Also claims that Randek was a stranger."

"Well, obviously, she knew nothing about tonight. Otherwise, she wouldn't have come in the first place."

"True, but if she was in league with Randek, and then he, or whoever he's in league with, tried to do her in as collateral damage, it stands to reason she knew something about their past activities. She claims she knew nothing. I think she might actually be telling the truth."

"So she's just looking at five years and the cost of the book, then?"

The Bordeaux Connection

"If that's how long the wives of MPs go to prison for. In any case, I got a message from Maria. Apparently, our orders are to sit tight till 08:00 hours."

"And what after that?"

"Await further instruction."

The Director completed his journey through Admiralty House, the corridors of the adjacent Old Admiralty Building and down the restricted lift that led to a quiet area away from the traffic. He used the secret knock on reaching the door and found Atkins, Maria, Phil and Jay all gathered around the round table.

Maria got to her feet. "Sir . . ."

"Get me the twelve on immediate standby."

"They're all out on active service. Hansen and Masterson are currently in Kent."

"Well, tell them to get ready. Tomorrow, each man is going to be needed for official deployment."

"Official . . ." She looked back in disbelief. "What's happened?"

"Turns out the old fool wasn't completely useless after all. He confessed everything, including the group's next proposed target."

Maria thought she was hearing things. "He confessed?"

"Put a call out to every man. I'm putting Operation Cockerel into action immediately. The location is Paris.

"The target: the Musée d'Orsay."

Paris,
00:23 Central European Standard Time, Friday 23 March

The train stopped at the Musée d'Orsay RER station at the usual
time. Unlike the trains that came before it, the carriages had an
empty feel about them. A sleepiness had taken over the station, a
predictable lull that always occurred between midnight and dawn.

Most of the passengers were getting on rather than off. Though
open until late on a Thursday, the museum had been closed for
over two hours, most of its visitors choosing to head home early in
preparation for a morning at work. Even the City of Light had a
bedtime on weeknights. A tourist hoping to fill the experience of a
lifetime living it up was more likely to get a warmer welcome
across the river. Though the station remained lit, the platforms
appeared almost ghostly in nature. The silence was disturbed only
by the gentle humming of the train, which became louder before
fading as the last carriage disappeared into the nearby tunnel.
Being a weeknight, this was its last call at the Musée d'Orsay.

The next would arrive after 05:00.

As the train headed east towards Notre Dame, the six men who
had alighted onto the platform did so with apparently little regard
for their surroundings. Four of the six carried bottles of lager or
wine, their faces suggesting they had enjoyed their night so far.
Nothing about the sight was particularly uncommon. If the reports
by the middle-class journalists were credible, the RER and the
Métro were renowned for such behaviour – the cause of it, even.
All of them fit the typical stereotype: all were male and a particular
type of male: white, well built, not young, but not particularly old
either. If the press generalisations were accurate, each would look
equally at home swearing on the streets outside the Parc des
Princes after an injury-time defeat to Marseille.

Or Bordeaux, even.

The Bordeaux Connection

Leading the six, two dark-haired men carried no alcohol, even to keep up pretences. The larger of the two was empty-handed, whereas the other had a soft cloth bag around his right shoulder. While the man with the bag was bearded, with thick stubble that matched the length of his hair, the slightly heavier of the two was clean-shaven. They looked at one another as they followed the natural curvature of the platform before heading for a door designated *Staff Only*.

The arrival would be by boat – that was what Pickering had told them. Aided by the natural cover of darkness, the would-be thieves would disembark on the south bank and make their way to the museum unseen. The execution of the plan was confidently expected to be without any significant problems. The security had been bribed, allowing a small window of opportunity. He didn't know how high the conspiracy went, only that it was high enough.

Whoever the boss was, he was not a man likely to be argued with.

Mike peered through his high-powered binoculars, taking in the south bank of the Seine. The eyepieces were not the same as the ones he'd used the night before; even compared to the opera glasses, the specifications were impressive.

It was after midnight, but not totally dark. It was Paris, and that was explanation enough. The City of Light was living up to its name. On both sides of the water, the illumination of the numerous buildings of architectural beauty lit up the night like a small galaxy. A gentle hum protruded the stillness: faraway cars driving the streets at various speeds towards an infinite number of destinations. For those used to the city, it was the sound of the city itself, one easily forgotten if you were used to it being there.

Among the noises, Mike could hear intermittent sirens: an unfamiliar high-pitched whining sound that reminded him he was no longer in Blighty. They reminded him too of other things: his first mission, another botched art theft, this time centred on the building behind him, whose famous glass pyramid reflected the light like an epic crystal. It also brought back memories of the films of his youth, the inspiration for his later career choice. Then there were also the holidays of his youth, weeklong stays in the cities of culture with his parents, siblings, and grandparents. His grandmother had once nearly lost her life in Paris to an ambulance, apparently heading on the wrong side of the road over one of the city's famous bridges. He smiled as he remembered before reminding himself of the most crucial thing the sound represented. The sound of crime. And chasing crime.

The reason he was there.

The boat had been hired in Paris. According to Kit, it represented a gentleman's agreement between the White Hart and a group of similar men whose origins were equally well hidden from the wider world. The boat was a small white yacht with the name *Suzanne* inscribed across the port bow. They didn't call it that. Like every boat in the fleet, its codename was *The King Richard*.

Mike lowered the binoculars and placed them down on the sideboard. Even without them, the main sights were easily visible. Across the water, the exterior of the Musée d'Orsay oversaw the south bank like a small palace. Like many buildings he'd seen recently, there was a sense of symmetry about the design. Two large towers rose above the main hall at either end, where two grand clocks commanded pride of place as if binary stars governed a miniature solar system. Light was visible from the windows, but even from the boat, he could tell it wasn't internal. The glass arches instead reflected the nearby streetlights like a dirty mirror. The floodlights caused the building to reflect off the water, creating a magnificent double image. It posed another timely reminder – one he knew might be relevant.

What exactly existed beneath the ground?

He heard footsteps to his right. Kit was walking towards him, dressed in his finest black ops gear. Like himself, he'd mastered a unique blend of being prepared without appearing suspicious.

The Bordeaux Connection

Kit stopped alongside Mike and leaned against the metal railing, his eyes on the water. "The boat in Peterhead was a cabin cruiser, once registered to one of Randek's companies. Interestingly, he apparently got rid of it as a tax write-off two years ago."

"A man who needs more practice filling in forms, perhaps?" Mike looked to his right, his strong blue eyes displaying clear scepticism. "You honestly believe he'd be stupid enough to use the same boat tonight?"

"No. However, if the Foreign Secretary is correct, a boat will be involved. If it were me, I'd probably arrive a different way and leave the boat till the end. If you're a professional art thief or a terrorist, you don't leave a boat parked where the entire city can see it. Nevertheless, based on events in Edinburgh, it stands to reason if they do use a boat, it'll probably be something similar."

Mike nodded. The logic, at least, was plausible; not that determining what was plausible was easy right now.

The last twenty-four hours had been hectic, though nothing new. The day had started early. The car had come to Chevening at 07:00, sent from Whitehall to collect the Deputy PM's wife. She left looking a picture of health, which was more than Mike had expected. The fully stocked wardrobe in the second largest of the house's 115 bedrooms had given her ample preparation for what he guessed would be a day of intense questioning, mostly about Randek. Even if Mr White didn't get the opportunity to grill her personally, he knew others would.

Including her husband.

Mike had left Chevening with Kit at the same time, their destination Charlestown. The briefing was done by phone, the rest on the helicopter. It landed at 19:30, thirteen hours after he'd risen from an awkward and interrupted sleep. The orders had been specific. Mrs Hughes was to remain under twenty-four-hour guard.

185

He lowered his eyes to the sideboard and sipped coffee from a flask. The wait had already lasted over four hours. Only one thing now was certain.

Nothing was certain.

The present building had originally been used as a train station. Before that, it had been a palace constructed in the 1800s on the orders of Emperor Napoleon.

And destroyed as an act of defiance against Napoleon III.

The replacement had been built at the turn of the 20th century as part of the Paris-Orléans railway. Randek had always loved how reference to its former use could still be found on the building's façade. The same was true of the names of the other cities through which the line had passed en route. Once upon a time, it had been the first electrified urban railway terminal in the world.

Even today, the lower levels continued to be used.

But even more important were the things no longer in use, things most people never realised even existed. One thing Randek had learned from history is that the last things to survive are usually the first things ever laid. The plans for the original building were kept in the Musée Carnavalet, including the outlines of the foundations.

Viewing them had been beneficial.

How do you stop someone who knows more than you and is operating two steps ahead?

Maria felt she'd figured out a way. If the Foreign Secretary was correct, their proposed route to the museum was predetermined. The target was one specific work of art; apparently, he didn't know which. If the heart of the plan involved cooperation with the guards, the best option was the most straightforward.

Get to the guards first.

Alone in a square room beneath the lower deck, Maria gazed unblinkingly at her laptop as the scenes continued to unfold. The infrared CCTV cameras placed at various points throughout the building offered her a complete view of the interior, including the logical exits. She arranged the display in blocks of sixteen, the images rotating consistently to allow constant updates.

The sights hadn't changed much so far. She often saw lights appear, a torch belonging to a night watchman doing the rounds. Neither Pickering nor Mrs Hughes had been sure of the likely target.

Even if Randek had achieved a guaranteed entry, he'd still have the cameras to contend with.

She heard a noise from the nearby doorway. Mr White had appeared, his features a picture of concentration.

"What's happening in there?"

"No change, sir."

"Keep watching. Remember, it only takes a second."

Musée d'Orsay
00:51

They entered from beneath the museum. Once upon a time, the area that was now the RER had formed part of an undercroft used by the palace governors to store supplies and keep prisoners. It was evident from the layout that the area remained in regular use, primarily by engineers ignorant of its historical pedigree.

Randek knew precisely where he was going. The original plans in the museum confirmed the architect's layout. Comparing them to the modern-day equivalent had been easy. Over the preceding two months, he had planned everything up to the last detail. It never paid to take chances, particularly with something so priceless at stake. Even at such a late hour, it was always possible an employee leaving late or on the night shift could turn up in the wrong place at the wrong time. The intelligence received two hours earlier confirmed every employee was scheduled to be off duty.

Entry through the first door had also proven easy. The next part would be more difficult. Darkness could help or hinder. Despite little chance of being observed, visibility was almost non-existent. They had entered a maintenance chamber that led through a gap in the foundation wall and onto the main track. Though the official timetable confirmed no trains were scheduled to pass by in the coming hours, walking the line with so little light made him nervous.

Two hundred metres further along, a second door appeared to his left, this one better concealed and cut deeply into the wall. On the other side, a metallic stairway rose at least three storeys; if the reports were correct, it headed into the museum itself. Everything had gone according to plan.

The way in was unguarded.

The Bordeaux Connection

At 01:03, Maria finally saw something appear on the screen. The movement had been slight, easily missed had she not been paying close attention.

It appeared first on Camera 16, a series of balaclava-covered heads moving in the darkness. They appeared again on Camera 27, then 19, 43, 56 and 73. Over the next minute, she saw movement on over thirty.

Phil was standing in the corner of the room, refreshing a flask of coffee.

"Get me the Director. Tell him we've got a visual."

Mike heard the call from his right. The others were heading down to the lower deck.

Mr White was standing on the deck with his hands placed against the small of his back, watching his men in quiet judgement as they lined up in two ranks of six.

"Our visuals confirm we're dealing with six. All are armed, and we can assume highly dangerous."

"Any familiar faces?" Kit asked, detecting a pause.

"Their faces were covered, but for now, we'll work on the assumption that they are. Your first concern will be to control the perimeter. That means twelve of you for each hour of the clock." He gestured with his hands. "Remember! The responsibility for the artefacts lies with the staff and the Paris police. Your sole responsibility is the capturing of terrorists. Do not confuse these duties. Good luck. And stay in regular contact."

Within seconds of receiving the order, four speedboats cast off from *The King Richard*, their rotary blades kicking up water as they sped towards the south bank.

Mike rested on one knee, his eyes fixed on the famous museum. He remembered visiting it years ago with his family; his father had toured the area at night with a tripod and an early digital camera, taking photos that would later appear in travel magazines. As a fifteen-year-old, deprived of a games console, a driving licence or a fake ID, joining him had been the easy alternative to staying in. His mum had never been much of a walker, particularly in foreign cities at night, and anything beat sharing a room with his brother and sister. Being the middle child was a strange position, especially in a family where no two people were alike. People from all corners of the world came to Paris for many reasons: the culture, the art, the women, the wine. His parents, he knew, had come for three of the four.

Others came only because their parents told them to.

He felt a hand on his shoulder. Kit was behind him, alongside Jay and in front of the driver. A fully loaded USP45 was in his right hand.

"Keep in regular contact. If anything goes wrong, get the hell out of there."

Mike was unsure whether he was experiencing genuine sibling-style concern or whether the instruction was strictly military.

"I'll be fine."

"I'm not talking about your health. Remember, there are more lives at stake than merely our own. And tonight, you call me Edward."

In keeping with every member of the White Hart, Edward was a codename – reserved only for one. Like his own codename, Grosmont, it was born of tradition. In the order's early days, the leader on the battlefield was the son of the king. Some referred to him as My Lord, others Cornwall. Many, the Black Prince.

Like his father, the king, he was named Edward.

"Yes, sir."

The four speedboats lingered briefly on the south bank as the twelve men of military stature disembarked and spread out around the nearest building. The Paris police had closed off the roads: surrounding the museum on every corner with signs inferring that roadworks were in progress. If a pedestrian taking a late walk had seen the twelve circling the building, there was no way they could get close enough to ask questions.

As the Harts disembarked, the drivers of the four boats turned on the water and headed slowly back towards *The King Richard*.

The Director of the White Hart watched the launch through his field glasses before heading below deck into the main office, where Maria was still gazing at her laptop.

"What's happening in there?"

For Maria, the last sixty seconds had proved surprisingly dull. "Someone has posted two men close to the entrance, both on the main stairs. He's also posted one where they came in and a fourth on the upper storey, possibly as a lookout."

Mr White watched the footage over her shoulder. "Zoom in on 25."

Maria focused on the entrance. One of the men was standing close to the reception area; the other was two steps up the main stairway that led down to the ground floor. Both were dressed all in black and armed with what appeared to be AK-47s.

According to Maria, the third man stood somewhere on the ground floor, where the intruders had gained entry.

The last man was on the top floor, an area abundant in paintings. He stood by a window that had once been an original feature of the former station. Maria didn't know the building well enough to decide whether the glass offered reasonable observation or was simply for show.

"Where are the others?" White asked.

Maria clicked the mouse rapidly, bringing a new window into view. Two masked men, she guessed Randek and Everard, appeared on Camera 42, admiring a work of art.

Maria instantly recognised it. "Albert Lebourg's *Paris, l'écluse de la Monnaie*."

"A valuable piece?"

"Absolutely, but I can think of better targets. Van Gogh's *Starry Night over the Rhone*, for starters."

Mr White turned away from Maria and spoke into his headset. "Edward. This is the King."

At the other end, Kit replied, "Come in, Sire."

"There are two shooters by the main entrance and another looking down from the windows. Proceed with caution."

"Roger that."

Kit passed on orders in a low voice as the men created a circle around the building, their frames hidden by nearby landmarks or parked cars. He held his breath as he felt the familiar adrenaline rush that came with the responsibility of his role.

Tonight, he was running the show.

Ten metres to Kit's left, Mike stroked the barrel of his USP45 as he gazed up at the arched mullioned windows in the yellow stonewalls. Despite the external floodlights, he could see nothing of the building's interior.

If the new intelligence was correct, the enemy was outnumbered two-to-one. Whether that was an advantage or not remained unclear. The reports from Edinburgh were that the Scots' numerical advantage had been five-to-one, yet the defeat had been catastrophic.

He heard Kit's voice in his ear. "Attention, north side. Possible shooters on the first floor and the stairs. Keep well covered."

Mike replied, "Roger that." His earpiece echoed as four others answered at the same time. He edged to his left, taking shelter behind a white van parked deliberately to give protection.

"I don't like this, Edward."

Kit looked at him. "You don't have to. All you have to do is stay where you are."

Everard stood alongside Randek, taking in the features of the painting. Though Impressionism had never been his favourite art form, he loved the way the city's famous outlines appeared through the mist.

The Bordeaux Connection

He approached the painting from the right side, awaiting Randek's instruction. Judging by its size and appearance, it would be heavier than most he'd handled recently.

"You might want to see this." Maria called for Mr White, who was currently in conversation with Atkins. Both headed for her immediately, the Director cutting Atkins off mid-sentence.

One of the masked men had cut the painting from the frame, taking great care to ensure no damage was done. Despite the lack of light, his actions guided by the single glow of the other's torch, the man seemed to make easy work of it.

"Needless to say, he's done that before," Atkins commented.

Randek took the canvas in his hand and slowly turned it over. The back appeared blank, as most were, the ghostly shapes of the main thing coming through as a mirror image.

Randek settled nonchalantly on one of the many benches placed selectively throughout the main hall. He nodded at Everard, who sat beside him, preparing to light a match.

"I don't like this," Everard eyed the nearby walls with deepening suspicion. "If a guard returns, we are done for."

Randek's balaclava failed to hide his fury. "If we fail now, the secret will remain unknown. We act now while we have that chance."

Once the flame went up, Randek placed it to two cotton swabs and brushed smoothly against the blank side of the canvas. Once finished, he rubbed his hand against the heat and blew on it.

"What is he doing?" Mr White asked.

Maria was speechless. The recent attacks had both involved explosions; now, one of them had lit a flame.

She watched on, quietly engrossed. "If I didn't know any better, I'd say they were exposing the painting to heat."

Randek couldn't believe his eyes. Even in the torchlight, the heat clearly had the desired effect.

He concentrated on the article before him, seated in perfect stillness. The patterns that emerged could only be understood with learned observation: the type he knew few were capable of.

Satisfied, he removed a small camera from his inside pocket and aimed it carefully, ensuring every inch of the canvas was captured. Then he repeated the process and looked at Everard.

"Good. That will do."

Mr White was baffled. On removing the painting from the frame and dabbing it with a heated swab, the man he assumed was Randek spent over a minute studying the apparently blank canvas before his accomplice opened the accompanying rucksack. He saw him remove something, a second canvas. Then something unthinkable happened.

They swapped over the paintings, returned the replacement to the wall and prepared to leave.

Randek had already seen everything he needed to see. If time allowed, they would explore the scene in more detail and in daylight. Nevertheless, the process had been useful.

If the painting really concealed the secrets he hoped it might, then the photographs would reveal everything.

Kit heard Mr White's voice clearly. "Edward, this is the King. The enemy is preparing to retreat. I repeat, retreat."

Kit bit his lip. Though the possibility had been discussed, it had previously been labelled unlikely. The battle plan had been to secure the building and wait for the police. "Where are the police?" He detected a delay at the other end as if the Director feared a miscalculation would prove unforgivable. "What are our orders?"

"Take everyone on the north section to the main doors. Once inside, you, Grosmont and Grailly are to advance to the ground floor. Everybody else, the upstairs. Maria will give you guidance. Everyone on the south side is to stay where they are."

Waiting in the wings of the gallery, the man by the windows detected movement close to the river. Though the sight of people wandering by the museum this late was not unheard of, something about the dark silhouettes through the glass caught his attention.

Randek was standing at the top of the stairs, relaying orders that the mission was over.

The man by the window waited until the last second before taking his eyes off the glass and following Randek to the escape route.

Musée d'Orsay
01:06

Entry into the museum was achieved with impeccable timing.

First, they unlocked the door, which required the help of a guard. Next came the deactivation of the central alarm, which had mysteriously already been switched off. To Mike, it explained Maria's story about a painting being removed.

It was still unclear who was responsible.

The opening of the doors preceded the quick movement of footsteps. Once inside, three Harts took the stairs up to the wings. Radio sets crackled with precision, the awkward tones of familiar voices ringing in Mike's ear. The upstairs had been deserted, the paintings, apparently, left untouched.

Mike followed Kit's orders. On passing through the central atrium, he took the stairway down into the heart of the museum, an open area with tiled flooring lined with art and 19th-century sculptures. Directly above him, the transparent roof was like a magnifying glass in the sky, its features partially obscured by dirt and pollution. Above the west stairway, another grand clock, similar in character to those that marked the exterior, displayed the time as 01:07.

The layout was easy to follow. Despite the regular presence of long, narrow benches close to the exhibits and often flanking minor stairways, the central aisle was wide enough for six people to move side by side without fear of damaging the displays. Even with the lights off, much of the interior was visible, again thanks partially to the architecture of the roof. Priceless artwork hung from walls on both sides of the gallery, the majority Impressionist. About midway along, Mike saw a sign to his right with a picture of Van Gogh's face and an arrow pointing to one of the upper levels. He recognised other pieces, one standing out above all others.

The Bordeaux Connection

Kit had crept up behind him. The purple light on his night-vision goggles had a bizarre effect on his face.

"*Whistler's Mother*." He recognised it instantly. "Should have known you were into Mr Bean."

On any other occasion, Mike might have mustered a smile. "This is all clear."

Kit spoke into his headset. "All knights report in."

Voices responded in rapid succession. "Upper floor clear." "Stairway clear."

"Edward, this is Beauchamp. Reception area clear. Heading for the offices."

"Roger that, Beauchamp," Kit replied. "Maria, what news?"

Back on *The King Richard*, Maria hadn't moved for more than an hour. "Lost visual eighty seconds ago. Camera 16 – same place they first appeared. Seems to be located somewhere on the ground floor. Head for the small stairway north of where you're standing."

"Roger that."

Kit grabbed Mike's shoulder and gestured for Jay, who was crouching, gun at the ready, close to a giant sculpture. Kit led the way to the top of a small stairway that led up from the lowest level to a second, elevated aisle whose decorations included a sculpture of an angel and the painting *L'Été* by Pierre Puvis de Chavannes.

Mike followed Kit up the stairs, his eyes moving from painting to painting. "Where are we heading?"

Kit bit his lip. "Maria, where to?"

The mission to infiltrate the museum and leave undetected had so far proven a success. Walking the hidden stairwell with his specially designed cloth bag and five companions, Randek was satisfied the security staff had been good to their word. Honour amongst thieves was a conundrum – especially in an industry where CCTV cameras were prominent, and reputation meant everything. Though he knew a CCTV blackout wasn't realistic, experience told him their identities were unlikely to be uncovered from the footage alone. They had taken every precaution. Every millimetre of their faces had been covered, as had the rest of their skin.

Everard stopped suddenly.

"What?" Randek asked.

"Listen."

Everyone stopped immediately, their footsteps shuffling. In the torchlight, sounds were difficult to pinpoint; judging from Everard's expression, he sensed something was happening higher up. The stairway descended from the museum's exit; eventually, it would lead back to the train line. Above, the noise of metal expanding sounded like a gas tank vibrating against a series of shopping trollies. Until tonight, Randek had never seen the stairwell first hand. He assumed it had been added to allow easy transportation between the museum and the station.

Randek looked at Everard, puzzled. "What is it?"

The cellist raised his hand for quiet, his ears straining for any evidence of sound. "I hear voices above."

Maria's instructions led them to the most logical of places. The escape had occurred in the north-east corner, an area with a stairway connecting to an upper floor and with signs for public toilets. Thanks to the security cameras, Maria could pinpoint the exact location.

Kit realised it presented one possible option.

There was only one door. It was marked *Staff Only* and was closed when they arrived. Entering, Kit found himself at the top of a metallic stairway, the type he associated with fire escapes and multi-storey car parks.

Mike entered next, followed by Jay, the features of the stairwell lit up by the lights on their NVGs.

Kit stopped before the first step and spoke through his headset. "Maria, I may need a satellite hook-up. We seem to have run into something unexpected."

"What?"

The Bordeaux Connection

"The door led to a metallic stairwell that only heads down. Follow it; we could walk into an ambush."

Maria had no definitive answers. "The building used to be a train station; the RER runs right beneath it, so it might come out near the station or on the line . . . how old is it?"

Kit knelt and studied the structure with both hands. "Mid-sixties, if I had to guess."

"Before the museum opened. Back when the building served as a hotel."

To Kit, that made perfect sense. "Just the sort of thing to help take in supplies."

"What can I say? In many ways, the building's history is as fascinating as its artwork."

"Let's not lose track of ourselves." He rose to his feet, the light above his face illuminating the features of his colleagues.

"Beauchamp, this is Edward. Follow my directions. I may need your assistance."

To Everard, the sound of voices was unmistakable. Not loud, but enough to carry. The voices were male, the language unquestionably English.

Instinct told him there could only be one possible source.

They were close to the end of the stairway, metres away at best. In the torchlight, the outline of the door was visible, its rectangular frame cutting into the wall like a primitive mine shaft.

Randek was standing at the bottom, preoccupied. He clung tightly to the strap of his bag and looked his comrades in the eye.

"You stay behind," he barked at two of the four. "Watch our escape. Whatever happens, this," he gestured to his bag that concealed the priceless artwork, "must be preserved at all costs."

The stairway descended the usual way: clockwise and in banks of four. Kit led the way; Mike and Jay brought up the rear. All proceeded with their NVGs set to night vision.

Beauchamp had joined them, along with two others. While the man, whose real name was Tommy Ward, was brown-haired and bearded, the other two wore far less facial hair. Each man was over six feet tall, capable of bench-pressing their own weight and confidently held identical PP-19 submachine guns. While Kit had known Ward since the latter's beginning, the other two were less newer additions. Beauchamp had spent the last forty-eight hours sweeping the rooms of Dorneywood and, after that, conducting a lone vigil at Gatwick for any sign of an Everard getaway. The others had done similar things both there and, later, Heathrow and Stansted. Their real names were Marcus Wilcox and Anthony Pentland.

Their codenames: Stafford and Salisbury.

A blaze of gunfire caught them unaware. Mike stumbled backwards, falling on the stairs.

He saw five bodies dive in different directions. Beauchamp and Salisbury rolled forward; Jay crouched close to the wall. Mike heard Kit shout something, Beauchamp something else.

Their words were inaudible because of the gunfire.

Mike put his hand to his night-vision goggles that had become lopsided due to his fall. Steadying himself, he edged backwards, carefully surveying the stairwell below. Kit was on one knee, the others on their front, guns raised.

He could tell no one was injured.

Further down, he made out features: two silhouettes standing at least two storeys beneath them. The gunfire resumed from below. Bullets ricocheted off the walls, causing sparks.

Thanks to the design of the stairwell, they were in little danger of being hit.

Kit was shouting again. Amidst the gunfire, Mike made out the words "Hold Back" before returning fire. A colourless blaze dominated his eyewear for over a second. Judging by the enemies' rapid movements, Kit's aim was close.

Mike retreated up the previous turn of the stairs, directly opposite Kit and Ward. The first thought that entered his head was

The Bordeaux Connection

of the impeccable mission the terrorists had carried out in Edinburgh. Twenty-four of Scotland's finest operatives had been defeated. Not killed but knocked out.

He removed a sleeping gas canister from his belt and threw it in the direction of the gunfire. Smoke erupted as the bomb bounced against the metal underfoot and away down the stairs. Mike followed it up with a second, landing within a metre of both men. Smoke dispensed immediately; through the cloudy veil, he saw them fall to the floor.

The gunfire stopped.

Kit removed his NVGs and looked up the stairs. For a moment, Mike expected a reprimand. In the end, Kit said nothing.

"Come on."

Kit was the first to reach the bodies. The men were white: one clean-shaven, the other more rugged. Both were dressed in black; Kit associated the type with his own profession. The guns they'd carried had been AK-47s, but that was only the crown of their arsenal.

He mused it would take a lecture from Phil to make sense of everything he saw.

The stairway continued in the same manner, clockwise and with no less than three levels. On reaching the bottom, a second doorway revealed itself; again marked with a sign that read *Staff Only*.

Kit smashed it open with his foot and dived behind the nearest wall.

Silence.

He returned to his feet and edged again towards the door, feeling it with his left hand. It was made of dense metal, heavy enough to close under its own weight.

He opened it again, this time slowly. The sight that met him was one of darkness. Reactivating the night-vision setting on his goggles, he made out features. The layout confirmed he was in a tunnel, probably beneath the ground.

"Maria, you were right. We've come out at the railway line."

Phil had been standing on the lower deck for over five minutes. With Maria on the laptop and no lab on board, surveillance of the banks seemed the only logical thing to do.

At 01:11, he saw movement. A boat had appeared from the west along the Seine. He estimated its speed at around eight knots. Using his field glasses, he identified a large cabin cruiser, its driver a long-haired scruffy man aged somewhere in his thirties.

As the boat came level with the Musée d'Orsay, he saw the driver kill the motors and glide safely towards the bank.

He spoke into his mouthpiece. "Maria, tell the King to get up here. There's something he needs to see."

Left or right – that was the call.

Kit faced his men in turn, ending with Mike. "Right, let's keep this simple. Grailly, you and Grosmont take a left," he said to Jay, referencing Mike. "The rest of you come with me."

Maria interrupted, words audible to all six. "If you head east, the next station is the Gare de Saint-Michel at Notre Dame. It's a solid two kilometres from where you are."

Kit placed his hand to his face. He estimated it represented an eight-minute run on an even surface for any of his men. He doubted Randek would take the risk on a train track in the dark.

"In that case, get Fitz-Simon and the others waiting on the other side. If Randek can't get out that way, they'll have no choice but to head back. If we can keep them in the tunnel, we'll sandwich them in."

Below the Musée d'Orsay
01:19

RER C had been dubbed the Museums' Line because it mainly served sites of historical interest. It officially opened in 1979 and had developed into the second largest of the five lines.

Within the city limits, the RER was identical to the Métro, sometimes faster because there were fewer stops. Each day, an estimated 500,000 people would climb aboard 530 trains, the last of which would depart just after midnight.

A time when the majority had already returned home.

The layout reminded Kit of the London Underground. Even though the station was closed, the platforms remained backlit, countless billboards showing up alongside vacant benches and vending machines. Again Kit took the lead. He sprinted across a deserted platform and headed towards the exit. Approaching the top of the stairs, he stopped in his tracks. The gated partition had been vandalised.

Allowing access to the streets.

"Maria, the gate to the RER has been breached. Suspects must have come out via the main stairway."

Maria typed on her keyboard. "Stay calm. Most likely destinations are east on *Place Henry de Montherlant* or west on *Quai Anatole-France*."

He emerged at street level, looking rapidly from side to side. Directly to his right, the main façade of the Musée d'Orsay lit up the night like a rising moon; to his left, *The King Richard* floated gently between the north and south banks. After being underground, the air felt bracing; the sounds of the city echoed in his ears. There was no traffic in either direction.

He remembered the road had earlier been cordoned off.

Maria leapt out of her seat and sprinted up to the lower deck. Mr White and Phil stood with their eyes fixed on the south bank. A white cabin cruiser had docked near the restaurant by the *Passerelle de Solférino.*

She looked on in disbelief as four men in dark attire sprinted towards it.

Kit's first thought was that Randek and Everard would seek to make their getaway by river. His instincts told him it was the most likely option.

As far as Mike was aware, they had never failed him.

He looked around in every direction. To his left, there were parapets alongside the pavement, separating it from a lower level. Over the side, he saw that a second road ran below it, with a handful of cars parked on the quay.

He scanned the river, right to left. A boat was docked almost directly under the bridge to his left, close to the *Restaurant Le Quai.* A second footbridge preceded the *Passerelle de Solférino,* crossing the road before descending in a spiral and ending near the bank.

There was movement on the nearest footbridge, four dark figures crossing it and preparing to descend the staircase.

Kit spoke as he ran. "Edward to King Richard, I have visual. Subjects are attempting to escape by boat."

Mr White didn't need any running commentary to know what was happening. For the last three minutes, his eyes had remained fixed on the boat, the cold of the metal railing barely registering against his leathery hands.

"I can see them myself, Edward. You're cleared to proceed by any means necessary."

Mike saw them before Kit. Wasting no time, he sprinted to his left, along the *Quai Anatole-France,* followed closely by Jay.

He estimated the drop to the lower level to be at least twelve feet – a risk on such hard ground, particularly with oncoming traffic. The road was dual-lane but one-way; headlights moved from east to west; cars passed by at speeds of over sixty miles per hour.

A locked gate filled a gap between the stone parapets. Mike saw it guarded a stairway leading down to the road below. His first thought was how – or why – Randek had missed it, but he quickly realised that it had been a wise decision. To head for the footbridge, though further away, led directly onto the quay, only metres from the boat.

If he took the stairway, Mike's only option was to cross the busy road.

Kit opened fire from above. Deciding against taking the first stairway, he sprinted towards the footbridge, stopped, inhaled, and steadied himself as he squeezed the trigger.

His target hit the floor immediately, his legs buckling beneath him. Taking a breath, he opened fire again.

A second hit; he guessed from the man's actions he was still alive. As he looked to his left, he saw Beauchamp had made it to the footbridge, followed by Salisbury and Stafford, both of whom were firing. Though the gunfire was audible, it was muffled, like a series of cars backfiring.

So far, it seemed to have attracted little attention.

He saw movement on the road below: two men crossing the rarely broken traffic. Moments later, he saw gunfire.

Coming from Mike.

The traffic was terrible. *It would be, wouldn't it*? Ever since the episode at the opera, Mike had sensed Sod's Law had it in for him.

The road was flanked by pavement on both sides; even on the left, it was wide enough to run along. Trees had been planted at regular intervals, their branches obscuring his view. Among the sounds of traffic he heard gunfire, apparently from above. He saw one of the thieves on the spiral stairway falling, then another. The other two were nearing the bank.

John Paul Davis

He recognised Everard from his superior size.

The traffic remained unchanged, prohibiting him from crossing. Cars were approaching on both lanes, their headlights blinding. Jay was following close behind, less than ten metres away and looking to cross.

As a gap appeared, Jay went for it, stopping on reaching the dotted line in the centre of the road and attempting to slow down the traffic. Mike held his breath and sprinted across. He made it to the other side and jumped the metal fence that separated the road from the quay.

Once over, he stopped, steadied himself and fired. The barrel lit up like a firework. Bodies moved on the bank. He saw the man he guessed was Randek jump aboard the boat, bag in hand. The man behind him began to slow, his pace little more than a stagger.

Finally, he collapsed to the ground.

Everard had never experienced pain like it. It felt like intense burning and freezing at the same time.

The first bullet had narrowly missed him. He saw sparks rise as they deflected off the stairway.

The second caught him on the right shoulder, causing it to seize up immediately.

The third entered his left hamstring. Though he could still move his leg, it was like a significant chunk of flesh had been removed. The first thought that entered his mind was that he would live and probably recover.

And that meant telling the tale.

Mike skidded to a halt alongside Everard, his gun pointed squarely at his forehead. He saw fatigue in Everard's eyes, different from the night before.

Behind him, the boat was departing. Its motor kicked up waves as it sped towards Notre Dame. Though he didn't recognise the driver, Randek was clearly aboard, his concerned eyes on his accomplice.

The Bordeaux Connection

"Where's he headed?" Mike grabbed Everard around the collar. Blood was pouring from the man's shoulder, staining his shirt and sticking to Mike's fingers.

Mike put pressure on the wound. "Where?"

Everard growled in pain. "*Eleventh arrondissement!*"

Mike released him and rose to his feet. Only metres behind him, Jay was standing with his eyes on the Seine; the boat was picking up speed, heading east towards Le Pont Royal.

Back on the footbridge, Beauchamp, Salisbury and Stafford were standing over the slumped bodies of the other men, both of whom appeared to be dead.

Mike scanned the footbridge, then the road above, realising someone was missing.

"Where's Edward?"

What's the greatest crime? The crime that occurred yesterday or the crime that occurs tomorrow?

Mr White's words echoed in Kit's mind. He had seen the two men he'd shot stumble to the ground; whether fatally or less seriously wounded, he was unsure. He saw Mike crossing the road, closing in on the bank. *Fair dos, the boy had chosen well.* Unlike himself, he had a chance of making it to the boat.

He made a snap decision. Heading in the opposite direction, he sprinted east along *Place Henry de Montherlant.*

"Maria, I'm going to need your maths skills. What's my distance to *Le Pont Royal*?"

Maria was standing on the lower deck, away from her laptop. "That's hardly maths."

"All right, geography skills then. How far?"

Maria eyed the bridge from the deck; its ornate arches were illuminated by streetlights. There were cars on the bridge, travelling south onto the *Rue du Bac* or north towards the Louvre.

She gazed back towards the Musée d'Orsay and tried to estimate the distance.

"I don't know, I'd guess four hundred and fifty metres," she said, confused by why it would be necessary. As she scanned the road alongside the museum, she noticed a figure sprinting east.

"Are you . . ." She paused as she spoke. "You're not going to do what I think you are, are you?"

Four hundred and fifty metres was just over a lap of the track. Kit remembered seeing Michael Johnson do it in less than forty-four seconds. He was no Michael Johnson, but he knew he was fast, particularly on the flat.

Better yet, no cars were in front of him to slow him down.

Keeping to the pavement, he sprinted east. He heard Maria break off before rephrasing the question. On this occasion, he decided not to answer.

It sounded like a rhetorical question, anyway.

The road forked after a hundred metres as *Place Henry de Montherlant* merged with the lower section of the *Quai Anatole-France* – the road Mike had just crossed. A pedestrian crossing connected the pavement near the south bank with the entrance to the museum. He crossed it at speed, pleased the Parisian drivers were obeying the rules.

Once over, he kept to the pavement, running alongside the river. As he looked to his left, he saw the boat had cast off, unsurprisingly heading east. He estimated he had twenty seconds before it passed *Le Pont Royal.*

He picked up the pace, grateful the pavement was deserted. As he reached the bridge, he saw the boat approaching; the sound of motors buzzed in his ear.

Fifteen seconds . . . ten seconds . . . five . . .

There was traffic on the bridge, heading both ways. Chancing it, he narrowly avoided contact with a silver Renault Clio and continued to the east side. As he got to the wall, he jumped.

And landed on something solid below.

The Bordeaux Connection

Standing below deck in the galley, Randek thought they'd hit something. His greatest fear was that they were in danger of sinking. He detected the crash had occurred near the front of the boat, somewhere close to the bow. Returning to the upper deck, he couldn't believe what he saw.

One of the Englishmen had made it aboard.

Kit landed within a metre of the railings that flanked the boat's exterior from the bow to the stern. As he saw the brightly coloured metal reflecting the nearby lights, he realised he'd almost lost a massive gamble.

Someone was standing at the helm, separated from Kit by a thick layer of glass. The driver was a tall man with both hands fixed on the wheel. Kit jumped the windscreen and crashed down on him. A punch to the face drew blood from his nose and lip.

The blow had knocked him unconscious.

Randek appeared in the doorway that led down to the galley. Sweat poured down his face and neck. He held a semi-automatic machine gun.

Kit fired, narrowly missing Randek's head. A blaze of gunfire ripped through the upholstery; the wilder shots created a line through the water. Randek dived inside the galley.

"You can't win this!" Kit kept low. "Your friends are dead. Return the painting, and we can talk."

Almost immediately, Kit heard gunfire coming from the galley. Randek reappeared at the doorway, a thick yellow blaze lighting up his firearm. Kit dived to his left, narrowly avoiding a bullet. As he returned fire, he heard speech; whatever Randek had said, the words were inaudible.

Randek fired until he was out of ammo and frantically tried to reload. As the gunfire gave way to silence, Kit took the opportunity to do the same and approached the door to the galley. As Randek's head reappeared above the gap, he kicked him hard; blood spewed from his nose. As he saw the Frenchman lose his balance, he felt hands around his feet.

They both crashed to the floor.

Kit rolled instinctively to his right, the gun still in his hand. He aimed to his right and sought to fire but stopped. The boat had drifted precariously inland, less than five metres from the bank.

He felt a presence above him, followed by a punch to the face, then another, causing him to lose his gun. As Randek reappeared, he rolled to his right, narrowly avoiding contact. The Frenchman's knuckles crashed against the deck; he cried out in pain.

Kit lunged for the wheel and turned hard to the right. He felt a crash, forcing them both off balance. He saw Randek stumble against the door to the galley, disappearing again below deck.

Kit went for his gun and pulled the trigger, his bullets further ruining the white décor. Randek reappeared suddenly through the door as his magazine emptied and jumped at his legs. Kit felt arms around his feet, bringing him to the floor. Despite landing on his left shoulder, the impact was worst at the small of his back, the area Everard had injured at the opera house. He felt another punch to his face, catching him square around the jaw, then a second just below his right eye.

He rolled to his left and struggled to his feet. Turning, he caught Randek with a right hook, drawing blood from the base of his nose. Two more followed, knocking the Frenchman to the ground as the boat surged forward, the impact throwing Kit against the wheel to his right. The boat was still moving, rebounding off the bank and back towards the heart of the river.

Randek was back on his feet. He kicked Kit in the groin and wrestled him for the wheel. As Kit tightened his grip, he elbowed Randek in the face, kicked him and raised the throttle. Again, he felt an impact from his left, another hard punch. He spun the wheel right; another crash as the boat's starboard side bounced against the bank. Stumbling, he felt a brutal force in the face. Blood dripped from his nose as he lost control of his legs.

The final impact took him overboard, head first into the water.

When he rose to the surface, he saw the boat accelerating away, heading east under the lights of Notre Dame.

Suffolk
12:00

Proceedings started early, despite a night of little rest. Mike had spent most of it on a helicopter, then in his bed in Charlestown.

It almost felt strange waking up in his own room.

Most of the stolen loot had been found in Paris. Thanks to Everard, they found it in the cellar of an antiquarian's bookshop on a cobbled street in the inner city. According to an inventory released by Interpol and the *gendarmes*, they included one by Sir Walter Raleigh: *The Ocean to Cynthia*. Also mentioned were seventeen items stolen from Edinburgh, including something called *The Flower MacDonald*, a clan text from the 1500s.

Apparently, it had been the most important target.

The news on Everard was much as expected. He'd been taken to hospital immediately, wounded but stable. According to the surgeon who had operated on him, the procedure had been straightforward. In the coming days, he'd be transferred to a high-security cell where he would await trial on terrorism charges.

Bail was out of the question.

The two Mike had taken out on the stairwell were still asleep by the time Fitz-Simon and the others came to tidy up the mess. Both woke up in a police car.

Both were now in custody.

The men shot on the footbridge were less lucky – or luckier, in Kit's opinion. Neither survived long.

Neither would face trial.

Mike was in his usual seat, his eyes taking in the familiar surroundings. Kit sat alongside him, the only other of the twelve present. It was approaching noon; outside, the sky was overcast, a light drizzle falling. The pub above, though open, was sparsely populated, which was usual at that time. Most present were the older generation, who often congregated in the lounge, playing dominos or chatting while watching Sky Sports.

All knew better than to poke their noses into other people's business.

Mr White approached from the far side of the room, his appearance immaculate as ever. Despite the pressures of the night before, his face displayed little hint of fatigue.

"The business in France, just like that in Edinburgh, must never be known outside this room." He walked in his customary slow and emphatic manner. His dark eyes focused on the famous table. "As far as the wider world is to be aware, the business at the Musée d'Orsay was the same as Edinburgh. An art heist gone wrong. The Parisians will never know whether anything was taken. Nor that we were even there."

Kit bit his lip hard. Though his back felt better, swelling around his right eye and nose confirmed his night had been eventful.

"Any news on Randek?"

"The boat was found seven miles along the Seine." Mr White raised his eyebrows and swiped his index finger across his electronic tablet. The large screen on the adjacent wall lit up with a photograph of a deserted boat set against a scenic backdrop neither Mike nor Kit recognised.

"Needless to say, both the painting and the man were gone."

"And the driver?"

"The entire ship was deserted. Two types of blood were discovered in separate parts of the helm. Of course, the possibility can't be ruled out that one of these was yours."

Quite probably, Kit said in his mind. "So the painting's gone?"

"I've told you before, Masterson, our only concern is the protection of the realm. If the museum wants to protect its wares, I suggest they improve their security. The *gendarmerie* already has three suspects. I think it's fair to say that the one that got away is already well known to them. It's only a matter of time before he's caught."

The Bordeaux Connection

Mike nodded. He'd been quiet, but not just because of fatigue. The three attacks had all been the work of the same people but carried out in different ways, for apparently different purposes.

The only definite connections were the person and the place.

Randek.

Bordeaux.

"How about the bastards who survived – I assume they've been questioned?"

Mr White walked towards the central console and returned carrying two items. "Everard confessed the crime at Edinburgh. Incidentally, that also helped establish a result on the book taken from Montacute House."

He circled the table and passed both objects to Mike. "I suggest you be more careful with these than I was with its doppelganger."

Mike picked up the manuscripts and examined the one on top. Though the title was barely legible, it had been placed in a file marked with references that only made sense to the staff of the National Library in Edinburgh. Inside, the content was handwritten, apparently of relevance to one of the clans of Scotland – the MacDonalds.

He had no idea what it meant.

The second was easier to read. *The Ocean to Cynthia*, also handwritten, apparently by a famous man. He opened it to the first page; the first thought that came to mind was of Shakespeare, iambic pentameter. Each letter was beautifully presented, making him wonder who the real Raleigh was? Great seafarers and calligraphers were rarely one and the same, particularly back then. As he skimmed the pages, he made out certain words. It was as if he were reading the emotional story of a man whose heart lay in another time and place. Like the ocean, the Tower of London's walls were restrictive, separating him from what he loved.

Who he loved.

As he neared the end, the writing disappeared, replaced by blank pages. On the very last, a few lines were visible, their shapes vague and random as if a drawing had been rubbed out. He looked at it for several seconds, hoping to identify a meaning.

Failing, he closed the book.

Mr White slid his finger across the electronic tablet, and the main screen went blank. "The Foreign Secretary will give his resignation speech to the Commons before the end of next week. News of his misdemeanours will, for now at least, remain classified. The reason for his leaving is a personal private threat against his person, coupled with the shock at having witnessed recent proceedings."

Kit smiled wryly. "So, as far as the world knows, he was the intended victim?"

"The Deputy Prime Minister, of course, has been cleared of any wrongdoing – not that he even knew he was under investigation. Charges against his wife are likely to be dropped as a reward for her complicity in exposing Pickering. As far as her husband knows, she was never involved. As I'm sure you're aware, that's how it must stay."

Both men nodded gingerly.

"Finding answers to the events in Edinburgh will continue – that and the attack on the opera house. With Everard incarcerated, only one man remains.

"Catching him must remain our top priority."

As Mike and Kit departed up the hidden stairway, heading back into the pub itself, Maria emerged from the far side of the room, her expression one of clear discomfort.

"You didn't tell them about the message?"

The Director eyed her briefly. "There are some things that are better left unsaid."

As Maria exited by the same stairs and headed for the car park, Mr White took a seat at the head of the table. He removed the white piece of paper from his pocket, unfolding it along the creases. The words had been handwritten, the penmanship precise. It was as if it had been written in the distant past when the

The Bordeaux Connection

words meant far more. Simply set out on paper, they amounted to nothing more than a short footnote in history. But to a man who lived a life few could ever understand, the sinister connotation was clear, a disturbing question posed.

How does Everard know the order still exists?

Mike savoured the first sip of his beer. Despite its true purpose, hidden from the punters in the room below, the inn also had an image to uphold. The local ales were famed among the regulars, particularly the old guard. Most enjoyed a good beer; tolerated a bad one.

These were among the best.

Kit sat on a barstool alongside Mike, his eyes low, his thoughts scattered.

"Oh, do cheer up. For what it's worth, you did well to even get there." Privately, Mike replayed recent happenings in his mind. He had been concentrating on Everard when Kit sprinted to *Le Pont Royal*. According to Maria, his attempts had been heroic. Worthy of commendation. If Mike had learned one thing in the last year, it was never the praise that mattered to Kit – not that he'd miss the chance of shoving it in his face. It was something far more personal – more real.

The villain still walked the streets.

An elderly gentleman from the lounge passed by, heading for the gents. He saw the bruising on Kit's face and asked, "What the hell happened to him?"

Mike grinned. "Didn't you hear, Freddie? His girlfriend caught him flirting with Maria."

The old man laughed and patted Kit on the shoulder. "You're lucky. In my day, it would probably have been a rolling pin."

Mike laughed, nearly choking on his beer. He looked around the bar, taking in the scenery. The locals were enjoying themselves, the old guard chatting with their former comrades, preparing for a fish and chip lunch to keep the hunger pangs at bay. As always in his visits to the bar of the White Hart, he noticed things on the wall: symbolism, trademarks of the order's past, scenes recognisable to historians worldwide. Things an outsider might see but never fully understand.

"I've always wondered. What exactly does that mean?"

"What?" Kit turned his head, his expression stern and swollen.

"That." Mike pointed to a painting of a white hart that decorated one of the far walls. Like many of its type, it was an original, its manner heraldic. Beneath it was what appeared to be a motto.

Honi soit qui mal y pense.

"Shamed be the person who thinks evil of it," Kit said, reading the line. "It's French."

"I guessed that. What's it mean?"

"The founder members of our order were once part of the Order of the Garter. The original Order of the Garter gets its name from an incident in Calais. Apparently, the King, Edward III, held a ball, and one of the ladies present, possibly his mother-in-law, had a garter slip from her leg. Whilst many in attendance sniggered at her, the King picked it up and returned it to her, saying those words. It's where the Order of the Garter got its name from."

Mike nodded, not fully knowing whether to believe it or not. The story sounded as though it had at least a degree of credibility.

He placed his ale on a beer mat. "There's one thing I still can't get my head around. The thefts all involved art and manuscripts, yet none were high profile. There were far more valuable things in Paris. Why a painting no one's heard of and manuscripts people don't even know exist?"

Kit sipped his beer and wiped the froth from his mouth. As he did, he shook his head.

"I don't know."

The Bordeaux Connection
Epilogue

Bordeaux
18:00, Central European Standard Time

The press had been covering the story since the moment it broke. Every news channel, from Euronews to Canal+, had focused on little else. Every station had a crew set up, usually two vans, if not three. The reporters changed shifts every few hours to keep things fresh, but only a few had gone home. Those who weren't on air were probably on the phone, be it to a contact, a potential source, or just to receive new instructions from the producers. Judging by how things were flowing, they were unlikely to go home anytime soon.

Most of the attention had been on the Musée d'Orsay, the scene of the crime – or attempted crime. The alarm had been triggered just after 01:00; the furthest the thieves had got was half a mile along the Seine, heading west towards a restaurant. As far as the police were concerned, everyone was now accounted for.

Almost everyone.

Walking the streets of a city over five hours south of Paris as dusk began to fall, Fabien Randek presented an air of purpose. On reaching a familiarly opulent street in the centre of the city, less than three hundred metres from the nearest stretch of the Garonne, he walked to the gateway of one particularly grand building and pressed the doorbell. As usual, the street possessed a sense of tranquillity, as though the buildings belonged to royalty. Being located so close to the river, the air felt refreshing.

The avenue itself was more expansive than most, the pavements on both sides shaded by the branches of chestnut trees that lined the way. The road was as famous for its gardens as its architecture. Like most on the street, the building was from the 19th century and could aptly be described as palatial. It was as if the road had been dropped in the middle of an arboretum. Should

217

a casual passer-by be driving past, heading for one of the main sights, they were unlikely to see much beyond the leafy vegetation. Like the famous borough of Kensington in England, privacy was assured.

A man emerged from within; he was bald and dressed in a fine suit, his physique clearly muscular.

He opened the gate and asked, "You are safe?"

Randek's expression was no nonsense. "The police are leaving. I saw them myself. They're moving across the water. Only the press remain."

"They are not looking for you?"

"No." He placed his hand against his bag. "But much can change."

The butler led Randek inside. Unlike his appearance of the night before, he wore an expensive suit with well-polished shoes that echoed as he crossed the marble floor. At the far end of the grand hallway, a fine circular stairway rose to the upper floors like a scene from a fairy tale. Priceless artworks lined its cyan walls, the scenes mainly relevant to the city. On reaching the second floor, the theme on the landing was the same. At the far end, a door was already open; Randek had seen it often enough to understand its unique significance.

He stopped outside and waited for the butler to announce him.

Finally, he stepped inside, taking in the sights he had seen many times. Within the great walls, illuminated by the natural light that entered from the original bay windows that commanded views all the way to the river, the setting was regal and businesslike. Twenty-four chairs surrounded the room's most important feature, a large table that dated back further than the house. Of the twenty-four, seven chairs were in use, all occupied by men seated together at one end, their facial expressions cold and serious. The first thing he noticed was the same thing he always noticed: the apparent similarity, not just to each other, but others also – famous others, including those captured in the paintings of old. While six were younger men, their ages

The Bordeaux Connection

indeterminate from forty to sixty, the person who sat in the position of prominence was considerably older, over eighty, his white hair and beard lacking its former vigour. He eyed Randek thoughtfully through thick bifocal lenses and cupped his hands together in deep expectation. To Randek, he was the boss.

As he was to everyone present.

"I must say I am surprised to see you. The news in Paris has been anything but pleasing." The coldness in the man's expression escalated. "Our family has too much at stake to risk failure."

Randek placed his bag down on the table. He unzipped it and revealed the content to his audience. After allowing them a moment to view the front, the elegant Impressionist artwork catching the light of the setting sun, he turned it over. While those at the table were too far away for the individual marks to make sense, Randek had seen everything he needed to see.

"The rumours, gentlemen, were indeed correct after all. The tunnel exists, just like they do in England and Scotland. The original ran from the Paris Temple into the heart of the Louvre."

"You have seen this?" The question came from one of the younger men.

"*Oui*. The same tunnel still exists now, hidden beneath the Métro. It starts in the same place and ends in the heart of the museum.

"In the bedroom once used by the King of France."

John Paul Davis
The Facts Behind My Fiction

As always, writing these books is a tremendous joy. Also, as always, the story was inspired by a mixture of fact and fiction.

Most of the locations mentioned in this book are real, and their descriptions are true to life. The Houses of Parliament are, of course, real, as is the Cabinet Office located at 70 Whitehall. Descriptions of the interior here, especially the Deputy Prime Minister's office, are made up – maybe one day they'll invite me inside! The Cockpit Passage, which connects 10 Downing Street to the Cabinet Office, does exist; my use in this book, however, is made up, albeit based on real-life descriptions.

The Admiralty Complex is a group of buildings located on Whitehall and close to St James's Park. Admiralty House exists, and its four storeys include three residential apartments used solely for members of the Cabinet, including the Deputy Prime Minister. The Old Admiralty Building alongside it also exists with parts dating back to the 1600s. There are rooms located beneath the ground, close to, among others, the Cabinet War Rooms. Their connection with the White Hart is made up.

Dorneywood and Chevening are actual locations, and both houses have been allocated to the Prime Minister for official use under the terms of their last owners' wills. The Chancellor of the Exchequer presently uses Dorneywood; during the Tony Blair government, John Prescott famously used it for croquet practice! During the coalition government, Chevening was shared by the Deputy PM and the Foreign Secretary.

The Royal Opera House is real, and references to its appearance and history are based on first-hand and second-hand research. I have taken a few liberties regarding the interior, most notably the smokers' section, which does not exist. I believe the descriptions of the auditorium and Paul Hamlyn Hall are accurate.

The locations mentioned in and around London are real; I have visited them all recently. The church of St Mary le Strand is real, and its inclusion in this book is inspired by my visit. The same is true of the Tube stations. There are vaults beneath the Royal Mile in Edinburgh; however, those mentioned in this book are made up. The chateau mentioned in Bordeaux is also fictitious. The buildings mentioned in Paris all exist, as do the RER stations. Descriptions and references to the Musée d'Orsay are accurate except for the hidden stairwell, which, as far as I'm aware, does not exist.

The manuscripts mentioned in this book are largely made up. *The Ocean to Cynthia* by Sir Walter Raleigh is alleged to have once existed, but no copy seems to have survived. The artwork mentioned is all real.

Charlestown in Suffolk does not exist, nor, of course, does the White Hart Inn and its secret room beneath the pub. The Order of the Garter is a historical order that still exists; the possibility that it got its name from the story mentioned in this book is a well-known legend. The Order of the Garter dates to around 1348 and was the brainchild of King Edward III and his son, Edward, the Black Prince. Five years earlier, the King made plans to create a special Order of the Round Table in honour of the Arthurian legends.

So far, no evidence has come to light that this order was ever created . . .

Acknowledgements

A book like this could never have been completed alone. I am most indebted to the kindness and assistance of many people. In particular, everyone I spoke to on my visits to London who selflessly offered me their time and expertise. A special thank you, again, must go to my fellow authors and friends, David Leadbeater, Karen Perkins, Mike Wells, Steven Bannister, Andy

Lucas, and Cathy (CR) Hiatt for helping to put *The Cool Box* project together, which included the first edition of this book.

Thank you for reading. Like every author, readers are the lifeblood of our existence. I hope you enjoyed the book. If so, please look out for my other titles, including *The Crown Jewels Conspiracy,* which takes up the current story:

Fiction

Standalone Thrillers

The Templar Agenda, 2011
The Larmenius Inheritance, 2013
The Plantagenet Vendetta, 2014
The Cromwell Deception, 2014 (a prequel to The Crown Jewels Conspiracy)
The Cortés Trilogy: Enigma, Revenge, Revelation, 2016

The White Hart Series

The Bordeaux Connection, 2015 (a White Hart prequel)

The Crown Jewels Conspiracy, 2017 (The White Hart #1)
The Rosicrucian Prophecy, 2018 (The White Hart #2)
The Excalibur Code, 2019 (The White Hart #3)
The Merlin Stone, 2022 (The White Hart #4)
The Lost Crowns, 2023 (The White Hart #5)
The Chaucer Manuscript, 2024 (The White Hart #6)

Non-fiction

Robin Hood: The Unknown Templar, Peter Owen 2009
Pity for the Guy – a biography of Guy Fawkes, Peter Owen 2010

The Bordeaux Connection

The Gothic King – a biography of Henry III, Peter Owen 2013

A Hidden History of the Tower of London – England's Most Notorious Prisoners, Pen & Sword History, 2020

King John, Henry III and England's Lost Civil War, Pen & Sword History, 2021

Castles of England, Pen & Sword History, 2021

Castles of Wales, Pen & Sword History, 2022

For more on me, please check out my official website, www.officiallyjpd.com.

All my books are available on Amazon:

UK Amazon Page

US Amazon Page

If you have any questions or you would like to get in touch, please feel free to email me using the contact me sections of my websites. You can also follow me on Twitter @unknown_templar and Instagram @officiallyjpd

Printed in Great Britain
by Amazon

61809757R00127